It was midnight!

"I'm sorry…good night, Patrick. I have to go!"
Catrina fled through the doors and into the lobby.

"Wait, Cat!"

"No. Patrick, I'm late.…" She pushed open the
outer door and ran into the humid June night. But
he was still behind her.

"Stop! You can't leave like this, when we've—
when I have no idea who you really are."

Cat didn't listen. *Couldn't* listen. Her skin was still
alive and hot from the way they'd touched. But she
had no illusions about what Patrick Callahan felt,
even if he did.

Skittering down the steps, she felt her spike-heeled
shoe come loose. It hurt. Why hadn't she felt that
before? Deliberately, she kicked the shoe off and
left it on the step.

Like Cinderella.

Dear Reader,

September is here again, bringing the end of summer—but not the end of relaxing hours spent with a good book. This month Silhouette brings you six new Romance novels that will fill your leisure hours with pleasure. And don't forget to see how Silhouette Books makes you a star!

First, Myrna Mackenzie continues the popular MAITLAND MATERNITY series with *A Very Special Delivery,* when Laura Maitland is swept off her feet on the way to the delivery room! Then we're off to DESTINY, TEXAS, where, in *This Kiss,* a former plain Jane returns home to teach the class heartthrob a thing or two about chemistry. Don't miss this second installment of Teresa Southwick's exciting series. Next, in *Cinderella After Midnight,* the first of Lilian Darcy's charming trilogy THE CINDERELLA CONSPIRACY, we go to a ball with "Lady Catrina"—who hasn't bargained on a handsome millionaire seeing through her disguise....

Whitney Bloom's dreams come true in DeAnna Talcott's *Marrying for a Mom,* when she marries the man she loves—even if only to keep custody of his daughter. In *Wed by a Will,* the conclusion of THE WEDDING LEGACY, reader favorite Cara Colter brings together a new family—and reunites us with other members. Then, a prim and proper businesswoman finds she wants a lot more from the carpenter who's remodeling her house than watertight windows in Gail Martin's delightful *Her Secret Longing.*

Be sure to return next month for Stella Bagwell's conclusion to MAITLAND MATERNITY and the start of a brand-new continuity—HAVING THE BOSS'S BABY! Beloved author Judy Christenberry launches this wonderful series with *When the Lights Went Out...* Don't miss any of next month's wonderful tales.

Happy reading!

Mary-Theresa Hussey

Mary-Theresa Hussey
Senior Editor

Please address questions and book requests to:
Silhouette Reader Service
U.S.: 3010 Walden Ave., P.O. Box 1325, Buffalo, NY 14269
Canadian: P.O. Box 609, Fort Erie, Ont. L2A 5X3

Cinderella
After Midnight

LILIAN DARCY

SILHOUETTE *Romance*

Published by Silhouette Books

America's Publisher of Contemporary Romance

SILHOUETTE BOOKS

ISBN 0-373-19542-7

CINDERELLA AFTER MIDNIGHT

Copyright © 2001 by Melissa Benyon

Visit Silhouette at www.eHarlequin.com

Printed in U.S.A.

LILIAN DARCY

has written nearly fifty books for Silhouette Romance and Harlequin Mills and Boon Medical Romance (Prescription Romance). Her first book for Silhouette appeared on the Waldenbooks Series Romance Bestsellers list, and she's hoping readers go on responding strongly to her work. Happily married with four active children and a very patient cat, she enjoys keeping busy and could probably fill several more lifetimes with the things she likes to do—including cooking, gardening, quilting, drawing and traveling. She currently lives in Australia, but travels to the United States as often as possible to visit family.

Once upon a time there were three sisters
who didn't believe in fairy tales....

For more than three years, they lived in a
run-down trailer park. Not many handsome
princes there. Things got better when they
found a fairy godmother—Pixie Treloar.
She had a house for them to live in. Still,
the sisters believed in their own hard work
more than they believed in rich men and
princes and knights in shining armor.

Then one sister, Catrina, met wealthy
Patrick Callahan at a society ball....
Would she learn to believe in fairy tales after all?

Chapter One

"**I** have located the target, Number One."

The deep-toned, disembodied words floated through the air like a silk scarf on a breeze. The hiss of skate blades across freshly resurfaced ice punctuated the sentence. An elegantly clad skater made a graceful turn, swished past Catrina Brown once more and said in a tone of even deeper significance, "Repeat, Number One, I have located the target."

Catrina, who was feeling nervous, lost patience.

"Jill Brown!" she hissed quickly, "Will you quit treating this like a spy movie and just tell me where he is? There's no one within five yards of us right now. Who'll hear above the music? And if by some miracle someone did hear, don't you think 'I have located the target' sounds just a teensy bit more suspicious coming from a waitress, than 'Would you care for a drink, ma'am?' "

Jill's face fell. "Oh...I was enjoying that," she said.

A neat flick of her hips scraped her blades sideways into the ice and brought her to a halt beside Cat. She balanced a tray of sparkling drinks in fluted glasses expertly in one hand.

"Well, I wasn't," Cat answered. "You've gotta help me blend in, Sis. That's your role. Pixie did a brilliant job with this dress, and that was hers."

Cat's sixty-two-year-old cousin Priscilla Treloar, known to everyone as Pixie, could sew like a dream. She had been the wardrobe mistress for a well-known national ballet company for more than thirty years until her health slowed her down and she'd had to give up work. She had insisted that the perfection of Cat's dress was one of the key elements in the success of this evening's plan, and Cat suspected she was right.

She fingered one of the dress's narrow diamanté shoulder straps. Apart from the straps and a matching diamanté edging around the bodice, the gown was plain black, and depended for its glamorous effect on the figure-hugging simplicity and perfect fit of its cut and line.

Beneath the full black skirt, the occasional peeks of layered silver lining were tantalizing. If you didn't look very closely, the imitation silk could have easily passed for a designer original. There were more than a few of those here tonight.

"My job is to be Lady Catrina, and I've got the aristocratic accent down perfectly thanks to half a lifetime of watching British sitcoms," Cat continued, her confidence rebounding a little. "I can do this. I know it. All you have to do is tell me which table Councillor Wainwright is sitting at, and I'll zero in. This whole thing is too important for us to mess it up by treating it like a game, Jilly. We can't have Cousin Pixie lose her home.''

The warmth in the way she used her mother's cousin's lifelong nickname betrayed the love Catrina and her two stepsisters felt for Pixie, even though Pixie was not a blood relation to Jill and Suzanne.

Jill had come back down to earth at Cat's words.

''I'm sorry. You're right,'' she said, then switched her tone suddenly as a pair of new arrivals at the Mirabeau on Ice ball came past. ''And I can particularly recommend the Mirabeau sparkling white....''

''Why, thank you.'' Graciously, Cat took a glass, as prompted, gripped the stem in her fingers and left her pinky aristocratically curled.

''He's at the corner table on the far side of the champagne fountain,'' Jill said, as soon as she was able to speak safely. ''With a group of several other people.''

''I'd better get on over to him, then.''

''Yeah, because he's not known for staying out late, according to our dossier.'' Jill grinned. Despite Cat's lecture, the word *dossier* had rolled off her tongue as if she said it every day. Then she looked guilty and apologetic. ''I'm sorry, Cattie.''

This time Catrina waved it aside. ''Just wish me luck, okay?''

''Oh, *huge* luck, Lady Catrina. Huge! This is equally important to all of us.''

''And you'd probably best not speak to me for the rest of the evening, unless you have to.''

''Gotcha. See you later, then.''

Jill swished over to a nearby table to offer her drinks tray as more designer-clad guests trickled in.

Cat was left with a tingle inside and a glow on her cheeks that she recognized as the effect of adrenaline. It wasn't nerves anymore but a buzz of exhilaration and confidence.

I'm going to be good at this. I'm going to convince Councillor Wainwright to vote against the proposed rezoning at the council meeting in August, and he won't have a clue this was planned.

She walked around the rink, using the carpet laid on top of the ice. She had to think herself into the role of Lady Catrina Willoughby-Brown, jet-setting member of the British aristocracy, and skates were a complication she didn't need tonight, since she wasn't the talented skater that Jill was.

The Madison County Ice Rink looked incredible tonight, a far cry from its usual mundane self. In the center of the rink was an enormous, flowing champagne fountain and some towering ice sculptures based on the works of famous artists—Rodin, Michelangelo, Moore.

Next came a specially erected polished and sprung wooden dance floor in the shape of a large O. A wide outer ring of ice accommodated the on-ice staff and any of the guests brave enough to put on skates. Finally, edging the rink were lantern-lit tables set on carpet.

The surrounding bleachers had been removed for the night to make room for platforms set with two more tiers of gorgeously decorated tables. The rink's floor-to-ceiling windows were frosted over with lacy patterns, and the walls were draped in black fabric.

Overhead there were chandeliers, mirror-balls and spotlights, all in the colors of Mirabeau wines, which ranged from pale straw gold through soft rose to a dark crimson. On a large dais at one end there was a band playing lively dance music.

Catrina shut all of this out, however, focused on her quest.

Yes, there was Wainwright, as Jill had said. Councillor Earl P. Wainwright, to be precise. He was seated with a group of six others, four of them men, at one of the best tables on the ice. Cat had her strategy mapped out in advance and she didn't hesitate.

First she waved to an imaginary acquaintance two tables farther on, then allowed her attention to be caught by the man sitting just to Earl Wainwright's left, as if in sudden recognition. Changing course abruptly, she bore down deliberately upon the total stranger. She had her brimming glass of Mirabeau sparkling wine in hand and a glittering smile plastered in place.

But then, unexpectedly, the stranger's eyes met hers for just a moment. Her hand jerked a little, and she spilled several drops of wine. He was already watching her, which she hadn't planned for. It almost shattered her focus. His strong body was draped lazily in its seat, and there was a tiny smile on his face, just tickling the corners of his mouth. For some reason she felt confused and self-conscious and...

Don't think about him, she coached herself quickly. He's not remotely important. He's part of your strategy for the first minute of this, that's all.

"Alasdair!" she trilled at him in her round-mouthed regal accent. She didn't let those dangerous blue eyes of his catch and hold her now. Instead, her gaze darted between a thick hairline, firm lips and a strong chin. "Fancy seeing you here! How marvelous! How absolutely marvelous!"

"Uhh...yeah," answered Patrick Callahan, CEO of Callahan Systems Software and reluctant guest at the ball tonight. "Marvelous."

He watched with appreciation and some alarm as a very shapely behind, clad in rustling black, slid smoothly into the empty seat beside him.

He'd had half an eye on the woman as she approached. Maybe a little more than half an eye, if he was honest. He was caught at this table by two or three people who might prove to be valuable clients for Callahan Systems in the future, and he was trying extremely hard not to be bored.

Trying hard, also, to understand *why* he found the prospect of the evening ahead such a chore. Most people would have looked forward to it.

Mirabeau was a California wine company that had hit on a novel marketing strategy. In several large cities across the United States, Mirabeau on Ice balls were taking place tonight. The buzz of publicity was deafening. By invitation only, the guest list for each ball was made up of an intriguing mix of the wealthy, the influential, the famous and the notorious.

Patrick wasn't quite sure how Callahan Systems had earned its pair of tickets. Having one of its founding partners, i.e., Patrick himself, named last year as Philadelphia's Most Eligible Bachelor by a well-known local magazine had probably helped. The fact that he'd briefly dated, in quick succession, both the Wentworth Hotels heiress and the stunningly glamorous ex-wife of a senator couldn't have hurt, either.

He would have turned the invitation down if his brother Tom hadn't reminded him of the networking opportunities. But he'd flatly refused to bring a date. He wasn't involved with anyone at the moment. He was never involved with anyone for very long. And the idea of creating expectations in some casual female acquaintance by inviting her tonight didn't remotely appeal to him.

No, if Tom wanted him to network, he'd prefer to attend the ball alone.

Somehow, the role of chief schmoozer at Callahan Systems had devolved almost exclusively onto Patrick over the past couple of years, since Tom's marriage. With their younger brother and business partner, Connor, also about to take on the yoke of wedlock in September, the situation would no doubt get even worse. For some reason, Tom refused to understand that events such as these were no longer a source of pleasure to Patrick.

Maybe that's because you haven't actually explained the fact to him, said an annoying little voice inside his head. Tom had no idea about the vague dissatisfaction Patrick had been feeling with his life just lately, nor the unacknowledged envy he felt for his brothers' rewarding personal lives.

"Okay, so if you don't take a date, you'll be able to cruise to your heart's content," Tom had predicted. "I bet Abigail Wakefield will be there, and Diane Crouch, Lauren Van Shuyler..."

"Cruise? I thought I was supposed to schmooze! Anyway, Lauren doesn't fit that category. She's a friend."

"Cruise, schmooze," Tom had said, ignoring the

issue of Lauren Van Shuyler. "You're a capable man. You can do both."

Subject closed, apparently. And now here he was, schmoozing on the outside while his inner spirit was a million miles away.

So he had welcomed the approaching lightweight distraction of this fair vision in black and diamanté at first, before he had any idea that she would stop at his table. But when their glances had connected just now, he'd felt something—a mysterious, intuitive quickening of interest. Not the sort of thing he normally admitted to, and it had spooked him.

"But I'm afraid you've made a mistake about who I am," he began. Why was he reluctant to disillusion her?

Then he saw that she had realized her mistake, too.

She clapped her hands dramatically to her mouth, then let them fall again. "Oh, I am most frightfully sorry!" she gushed. "I thought you were Alasdair Corliss-Bryant, an old friend of mine from the Gloucestershire Hunt. But I can see now that of course you're not."

"I'm sorry to disappoint you," Patrick answered.

It was a formula response. He was aware that, on his left, local councilman Earl P. Wainwright, one of his schmoozing options for the evening, was now listening with eager attention to the new arrival. Hardly surprising. Miss England was gorgeous.

Patrick made a cool-headed assessment.

Maybe not quite as cool as he would have liked.

She was about thirty-five years too young for Wainwright, but that didn't seem to concern the man. Untamable blond hair framed her face, and her eyes shone like brown sugar melting with butter in a hot skillet. She had long lashes, a glove-tight dress, full lips and a fabulous figure.

Of course, he'd seen it all before, Patrick quickly decided. Of course he had! He'd seen it bigger, better and sexier.

Still, he was intrigued. Not by the packaging but by the motivation. No one else had been watching her performance as she sashayed past. That it was a performance, and not at all genuine, Patrick was already quite certain. And this made him wonder about a few things.

Why, for example, had she pretended to recognize him? That recital about Alasdair Double-Barrelled-Moniker and the Whatsit-shire Hunt was too complicated. He was annoyed that she had chosen such a strategy. Overly elaborate. Unnecessary.

He frowned.

Wouldn't it have been a lot simpler just to trip over the carpet and lunge at his knee? A woman like this surely wouldn't begrudge a spilled glass of champagne and a dry-cleaning bill for his suit in a good cause, would she?

And why the phoney British accent? It was good. Very good. None of the vowels had slipped. Still, he was in no danger of believing it to be genuine. He'd learned in business never to take anything at face value. So…why?

He considered the issue, enjoying the fact that his mind was engaged now.

Presumably it was the Most Eligible Bachelor thing. He regretted the publicity that had given him, now. There had recently been a couple of how-to books written expressly for gold diggers. Maybe this was all written down in black-and-white in chapter four. "Capture his attention by pretending to be a card-carrying member of the British aristocracy." Lady Catrina Willoughby-Brown was the name she'd selected for the evening, apparently.

He examined his options with a degree of relish. Challenge her at once? She deserved it, but for some reason he was tempted to play along with her game.

He had just decided on this second option when he made a very disconcerting discovery. Astonishingly, he, Patrick Simon Callahan, aged thirty-six, with a net worth upwards of twenty million dollars and still climbing, and a not-insignificant quantity of personal appeal as well, was not Lady Sugar-Eyes's target at all.

"Councillor Wainwright, I'm so pleased to meet you," she gushed, ending the round of formal introductions. Patrick hadn't paid much attention to any of it until now. He slumped back in his seat, pushed aside by the sheer force of her determination.

"Lady Catrina, it's an honor," the councillor replied earnestly. "I love your country. I visit England every chance I get. In fact, you may know some friends of mine..."

"Oh, really? How marvelous!"

She was leaning past Patrick. On display was a tastefully moderate yet very alluring quantity of silky-skinned cleavage. Fixing her warm, liquid brown eyes on Councillor Wainwright, she nodded encouragement at the man's words, denied knowledge of his old friends, and offered some no doubt fictional names of her own. Lord Peter Devries? The Honourable Amanda Fitzhubert?

For some reason, the very appealing effort that

she was putting into hunting completely the wrong quarry immediately irritated Patrick up to the eyeballs. What was it that mom had drummed into him and his seven brothers as children? It had been one of the more annoying sayings of an otherwise excellent and well-beloved parent.

"If a job's worth doing, it's worth doing well."

He now discovered to his horror that he agreed wholeheartedly with these prim words of mom's. If a woman was going to be a fortune hunter, if she'd gone to all the trouble of shimmying herself into that delectable, form-fitting dress, gate-crashing this event, inventing an upper-crust identity, perfecting the accent and wangling an introduction, then she should at least be good at it. She should aim high. She should choose the right man.

Him.

Leaving aside any other considerations, such as age, physical endowments and suitability of temperament, Patrick was streets ahead of Councillor Wainwright where it really counted to a woman like this.

In the bank.

It wasn't that Patrick himself measured his masculinity in financial terms. He didn't come from a moneyed background, but from a good, solid family in which other values—honor, love and Christian charity—took precedence.

Occasionally he was cynical about those values, but deep down he believed in them. He'd started to realize just lately that one of the reasons he still wasn't outrageously in love and blissfully married like his brothers Tom, Adam and Connor, was because he just couldn't respect or love a woman to whom money and possessions and regular appearances in magazine gossip columns were the be-all and end-all.

The pity of it was that when you were widely known as a rich young gun in the world of computer commerce, you attracted such women—beautiful and sophisticated women, many of them—in droves. The fictitious Lady Catrina was clearly one of them. That was strike one against her. The fact that she was doing it *all wrong* was strike two.

So there was no excuse at all for what Patrick said next.

"Would you like to dance?" His abrupt question cut right across the honeyed conversation taking place between Earl Wainwright and Lady Catrina.

The latter turned to him with a frown. As well she might. His interruption had been extremely rude.

Still, Patrick was astounded to hear himself apologize. He felt his neck grow hot inside his collar. "I'm sorry. When you've finished your conversation, of course."

"No, no…!" Wainwright waved a paternal hand. "Take her, my dear old chap." Like cheap gilt, some of the fake accent and British vocabulary had rubbed off on him.

"Please, Councillor Wainwright, do finish your story," Lady Catrina cooed.

She hadn't even glanced at Patrick, who was now pressed hard against the back of his seat by her single-minded determination to lean across him. Her bare, lovely shoulder was turned to him, so close that he could have nuzzled it with his lips if he'd wanted to.

Not that he did, he reminded himself.

"Heavens, no, Earl! The story's not very interesting," said one of the women farther around the table. She was watching Lady Catrina suspiciously. "Do go and dance, you two!"

The woman was dressed magnificently in chartreuse beaded satin, and her cheeks were rosy-bright from champagne. She looked to be about fifty-five, and it suddenly clicked. For heaven's sake, this was Darlene, Earl Wainwright's wife!

Patrick wanted to coach his gold-digging, pseudo-British friend, "Get real! Sheesh, woman! You can't make a play for the man in front of his own wife!"

Perhaps Lady Catrina had realized this herself. Trying unsuccessfully to disguise her reluctance, she stood up.

"Dancing! How splendid!" she exclaimed unconvincingly. She tossed a frown back at Earl Wainwright, then apparently accepted the inevitable and took a step towards the ice.

Patrick glanced down at her spiky black heels. "Better take my arm, I think. We have to navigate that ice."

"There are escorts for that," she told him absently. "On skates. Here."

She reached the edge of the carpet and was joined by a bladed male. A skate bunny took Patrick's arm and helped him skitter across to the comparative safety of the wooden dance floor. Now he was face to face with her, and the music was slow. He took her into his arms.

Inwardly, Cat was still cursing the stranger. What had he said his name was? Patrick something. Callahan, that's right, "Managing Director of Callahan Systems Software," someone had said.

It wasn't important. The only reason she'd accepted his invitation to dance was because it would have drawn too much attention if she hadn't. She certainly didn't want to upset innocent Mrs. Wainwright any more than absolutely necessary.

She tallied up the details of Patrick Callahan's incredible good looks with less warmth than she'd have shown in assessing the shape and size of a Christmas tree in a wintry sale yard. Yeah, sure, he had it all. The height, the build, the hair, the shoulders, the Grecian nose and jaw, the healthy tan on his skin, the air of confidence, assurance and bone-deep entitlement.

He was the kind of man she detested, no doubt about that. An upmarket version of how Barry Grindlay must have been fifteen or twenty years ago. Barry Grindlay, the sleazy developer who was poised to bulldoze sweet, frail Cousin Pixie's family home the moment the rezoning of lower Highgate Street went through in the middle of August. Barry Grindlay, who had no intention of paying Pixie market value for the place if he could possibly help it. Barry Grindlay, who refused to accept the fact that Pixie didn't even want to sell in the first place.

In other words, Patrick Callahan was...had to be...arrogant and totally ruthless in his wealth and good looks. He had that sense of unquestioning entitlement written all over his face. He was the type who'd do anything for money, Cat was quite sure. And he undoubtedly believed that money could do anything for him, including pick up any woman he wanted, close any deal he wanted, buy any opinion he wanted.

In contrast to Grindlay, however, the CEO of Callahan Systems Software wasn't important enough in Cat's life to take the trouble of loathing. All she had to do was get this dance over and done with as smoothly as possible.

Doable. Easy.

He took her hand and held her in the middle of her back, and they began to waltz. Cat was thankful for Jill and Pixie's dance lessons over the past couple of days. Patrick Callahan had done this before. He didn't make the clumsy man's mistake of trying to cover too much ground at once. They just pivoted gently in one spot, in three-four rhythm, leaving him plenty of time to gaze intently into her eyes.

Which, for some reason, he seemed keen to do.

They didn't talk at first. Cat had to concentrate very hard in order not to start muttering, "*one,* two, three, *one,* two, three," under her breath.

Patrick's eyes were mesmerizing, she soon discovered. They were bluer than the reflection of a clear summer sky in a mountain lake, blue enough to put both Mel Gibson and Paul Newman into serious therapy. And there was a warm and very appealing glint of curiosity in them that drew her own gaze.

It made her want to ask, "Why are you looking at me like that?"

Since she refused to express any interest in the man whatsoever, she didn't say it. Instead, each time they circled, she craned her head to glimpse Earl Wainwright to make sure she didn't lose track of him. It was frustrating at first.

If only I was dancing with the councillor instead...

But then Patrick eased her a little farther out onto

the floor and other bodies got in the way. Cat couldn't see Councillor Wainwright anymore. She suppressed a sigh, surrendered her impatience for the moment and hoped desperately that the dance would end soon.

Chapter Two

Patrick felt the stifled movement of Lady Catrina's sigh, and his curiosity surged once more.

Her body had been quite a distraction. There was something about this woman. She was lithe, supple and smooth in his arms. Her body was slim but strong and healthy. There was a warmth and sparkle to her that he hadn't expected to find, an aura about her that suggested she lived her life to the fullest.

He couldn't put his finger on it. Did it come from her eyes?

Well, no, apparently not. When they rested on him, they were cool and bored, and when they moved elsewhere, they were frustrated and impatient, which gave him a sour sort of feeling in his gut that he couldn't quite identify.

His hand rested against the black fabric at the back of her simple, swishy dress. He could tell it wasn't silk. Her skin would undoubtedly feel much, much silkier. He was a little startled to catch himself in the wish that the back of the dress was lower, so that he could discover the texture of her skin with his fingers.

Was he attracted to her, then, despite his cynicism?

Hell, yes! And he couldn't understand why he didn't have more control. He'd already decided exactly what sort of a person she had to be, and he wasn't impressed.

All the same, there were things about her that didn't fit...like the scratchy feeling on the heel of her hand, another item on a growing list of things he hadn't identified yet. What on earth was that?

And this gown intrigued him. The fabric was cheap, yet his eye told him the gown was beautifully made, fitting her like a designer original stitched by a professional to her unique measurements. And that was a contradiction, because if she could afford a made-to-measure garment, why couldn't she afford silk?

Since this was a far safer issue than the complicated matter of his unwilling...and growing... attraction to her, he focused on it and began to challenge her subtly.

"I hadn't expected to come across a certified member of the British aristocracy at this event," he murmured. "What brings you to Pennsylvania?"

"I'm staying with some friends," she said, without hesitation. Without blinking, either, he noticed.

"They're here tonight?" He knew they wouldn't be.

"No, they were ill at the last minute and couldn't come."

Yeah, right!

"How sad!"

"Yes, it was a frightful pity."

"Frightful," he agreed.

"So I'm here on my own."

"Where did you meet these friends? Here in the U.S.?"

"No, in Gstaad last winter. We were all there for the winter sports."

"Gstaad? I didn't think anybody went there anymore," he commented. He was making this up on the spot, knew only that Gstaad was a winter resort somewhere in Switzerland, but he wasn't disappointed in her reaction.

"Oh, well, I know," she answered far too quickly, and he couldn't help appreciating the agile movement of her mind. "But of course, um, that's its great advantage. One simply can't stand to be crowded into some too-too fashionable resort where everyone only goes to be seen."

"No, I imagine *one* would find that very trying," he said. If she had picked up on his parody of her accent and word choice, she didn't let on.

The music ended, and he felt her begin to pull out of his arms as if she couldn't wait to get back to Wainwright. Afraid of being found out?

Pretending not to notice her movement, he tightened his arms around her and said very smoothly, "We'll have another one, shall we? The night's young yet. Plenty of time to..." Deliberately he trailed off, and she fell into the trap.

"To what?" she said.

"I was hoping you'd tell me."

"I—I don't understand."

"No?"

He shrugged, in no hurry to get to the point. It was much more interesting to do this *slowly*. The music began again, another waltz. On the ice, professional skaters were whirling around in glittering costumes with flaring skirts. A faint mist arose from the cold white surface.

On an impulse, Patrick asked her, "So, what do you think of the way they've set all this up tonight?"

"Oh, they've done a terrific job, don't you think?" she answered at once, and her face lit up. The accent got a little wobbly, but she didn't notice and he didn't care. Her eyes were warm, dark pools and her cheeks were pink.

"The whole thing's incredible," she continued. "I could never have imagined they'd make it look so good, when it...uh...must normally be so bland. They must have worked incredibly hard. The sculptures are beautiful, and the lights, and the costumes. And I hate to think who was up on ladders for hours frosting all those patterns on the glass. I love it!"

"But of course you've attended this sort of function many times before," he reminded her gently, knowing perfectly well that she hadn't.

Jaded jet-setters didn't express such enthusiasm in his experience. Nor did they spare a thought for the anonymous workers who had toiled to prepare their pleasures. He'd never met one who wasn't entirely and selfishly oblivious to such details.

So who was she?

She didn't seem like a fortune hunter. There was a sincerity about her...which was a ridiculous word to choose when even the name she'd given him was phony. She had to be about as sincere as a computer-generated telephone message.

"Oh, of course," she was saying quickly, the accent back in place and more plum-in-the-mouth than ever. "But this actually compares rather well to the Ascot Ball, and…uh…and so forth. I'm pleasantly surprised." She faked a well-bred yawn behind her hand, then shot a little glance up through her lashes to gauge his response.

He had to hide a smile. Hell, she was a cute little liar!

Is that champagne going to my head? he wondered.

It was a long time since he'd enjoyed dancing this much. Normally, it was something he put up with. He considered it a matter of business etiquette if the occasion was professional, or a form of foreplay if it was private. But tonight…with her…it felt great.

"I like the dinosaurs, by the way," he said.

"The—? Oh. Right." The tip of her tongue darted nervously to the corner of her soft, lovely mouth, and she gave a jerky little nod.

He hid another smile of satisfaction and amusement. He'd managed to identify the scratchy feeling on the heel of her hand, finally. A Band-Aid. Just now, he had sneaked a look and had discovered that it was the kind made for children, printed with red, blue and yellow dinosaurs.

Another tiny clue as to who she really was, another thing to pique his interest. Wearing a Band-Aid like that, she had to spend a lot of time with kids. It didn't fit the character she was trying to portray, and she knew it, which accounted for her nervous reaction to his discovery. Strangely, it didn't seem to fit the fortune-hunter stereotype, either.

"Will you be staying long?" he asked now.

"No, I don't expect so," she said quickly. "I'll leave as soon as I can. I have to, uh, be somewhere else later in the evening. You know, one's busy social whirl."

"You're talking about the ball. I meant staying in Philly."

"Oh. Right," Cat repeated thinly.

Drat! Again!

It was as if a cloak had slipped. She gathered her artificial role around herself once more and cursed the dropping of her guard. It kept happening, when she'd been so confident that she had it down pat. There was something about Patrick Callahan that was way too distracting.

And he was way too observant, as well. That darned Band-Aid! Yesterday evening, she'd cut her finger at the twenty-four-hour child-care center where she worked, slicing some fruit for the kids' late-night snack. She had meant to exchange the dinosaur Band-Aid for a plain one today, but had forgotten in the flurry of getting ready.

"How silly of me!" she trilled with an effort. "Of course you meant this wonderful city of yours. But I'm afraid I'm leaving tomorrow."

"Somehow I thought you might be," he murmured. "Flying first-class?"

"Naturally. To Paris."

"Wonderful. Where do you usually stay when you're there?"

"Oh, just an exclusive little hotel downtown." She gave a vague wave, which accidentally brushed his neck. It was warm, and suddenly she caught the waft of a musky male scent, a mixture of him and his soap, released by the brief brush of her fingers. "You wouldn't know it," she finished hastily.

"Probably not," he agreed. "Interesting, though. I've never heard anyone refer to Paris as having a 'downtown' before."

"No, well, I didn't know if you knew the city or not," Cat said, trying to infuse a note of arrogant condescension into her tone. Paris didn't have a downtown? How was she supposed to know that, since she'd barely been out of Pennsylvania?

The man was really starting to make her nervous. That glint in his eye. That little smile that came and went in his face. It drew her attention far too often to his extremely kissable mouth.

Yikes, no! *Not* kissable! Good gosh! Note to self: *No more Mirabeau champagne tonight!*

"*I* know Paris," he was saying. "I was wondering if you do."

"Well, of course I do!" she claimed, then added with sketchy logic, "Didn't I just say I'm about to go there?"

"So you did." Again, he smiled at her, creasing all the tiny laugh lines on his face in a way that made him look far less intimidating, far more human. Then he slowly pulled her closer so that she had no choice but to rest her head against his shoulder as they danced, and there was that fresh, musky scent again.

She could feel his legs, now, getting tangled in the layers of her dress, and his arm was no longer safely in the middle of her back but much farther round, in the curve of her waist, just below her breast. As they moved, she could feel the weight of her fullness there, nudging softly against his hand. It didn't feel anywhere near as unwelcome as she wanted it to, and she was melting inside. Was he flirting with her?

A silence fell. She would have spoken, only she was too afraid of saying something that would betray herself to him, too afraid that she had betrayed herself already.

Darn it, she knew she had! He had guessed who she was—or at the very least, who she *wasn't*—and he was playing along with her.

Instead of hating him for it as she should, she found herself responding at first. Responding to that little half-smile of his, as if they shared a delicious, creamy, edible secret, instead of a secret that could blow her whole plan to smithereens if he revealed it to Councillor Wainwright.

How much, exactly, did he know? The detailed truth about who she was? Surely not!

Not the fact that she'd been kicked out of her home by her mean-spirited stepmother Rose six years ago, the moment she hit eighteen. Not the fact that her stepsister Jill, almost the same age, had been kicked out right along with her because Jill was pregnant and unmarried and the baby's well-heeled, well-connected father didn't want to know about it.

Not the fact that Jill's older sister Suzanne had refused to remain in a house where her sisters weren't welcome, so that all three of them, plus Jill's little son Sam, had ended up struggling to survive in a no-hope trailer park for several years.

Yes, a trailer park, and not the kind where the

other residents troubled to grow flowers and put drapes in their windows.

Thanks to Cousin Pixie, that life was behind them now. Cat was well on the way to completing her nursing degree and she was loving it. After turning her back on a career as a show skater following a disastrous six weeks in Las Vegas earlier in the year, Jill was training in computers and administration while she worked in the ice-rink office part-time. Infiltrating tonight's ball under deep cover had been her idea. Suzanne had recently gotten her degree in library science. They each had hopes for the future. Still, they counted their pennies every single day.

Patrick Callahan knew Cat had as much right to call herself Lady Catrina Willoughby-Brown as she had to claim she could fly. But did he know how important this evening was to her? Did he know it wasn't a game or a scam? Did he know that she and Pixie, Jill, Sam and Suzanne would all lose their home if he blew her cover tonight?

Of course he didn't, and even if he did, if he'd somehow guessed why she was targeting Councillor Wainwright so assiduously, she doubted that he'd care. His type never did. From bitter experience, she knew this all too well.

There was a whole roll call of such people who'd impinged on her life. Curtis Harrington III, the Ivy League college boy who'd fathered Jill's son. Barry Grindlay and his ruthless devotion to the bottom line. Her stepmother Rose, too, had given Cat many an unintentional lesson about the gulf that separated the privileged and the strugglers of this world.

The dance came to an end at last. Patrick led Cat from the floor, his fingers linked loosely through hers, and she was so relieved that this was ending that she didn't spot his intention until it was way too late.

He'd taken her back to Earl Wainwright's table and suggested cheerfully to the councillor, "That was fun. Why don't you and Mrs. Wainwright take a turn now? There are a lot of couples out there now."

Mrs. Wainwright's eyes instantly lit up. "Oh, Earl. Why don't we? He's right. It isn't just young people, and they're playing our sort of music."

Seconds later, Cat had to watch her elusive quarry stumble across the ice under the escort of a seventeen-year-old skate bunny. Patrick sat back in his seat, meanwhile, openly enjoying her poorly disguised chagrin.

"They're serving more supper," he said, then gestured at Jill, who was swishing by with a tray of filled plates.

She came to an elegant halt—she really was a beautiful skater!—and laid two plates down in front of them with a beaming smile. This quickly turned into a confused glare at Cat when she thought Patrick wasn't looking.

Why are you wasting your time with this guy? the glare said.

Cat gave a tiny frown back and shook her head, as if to say, "Believe me, I'm trying to shake him off!" then Jill swished away with her tray once more.

"She skates well," was Patrick's comment.

"Yes, she does, doesn't she?" Cat began warmly, then corrected her tone quickly. "That is to say, she seems more skilled than most of the people one sees on the outdoor rink at Gstaad.''

''Ah, we're back to Gstaad,'' Patrick murmured.

He tortured her without mercy as they ate. Cat hated herself for appreciating every moment of his cleverness. Never once did he say straight out that he knew she was a fraud. That would have been too easy. But he broke her cover again and again.

He trapped her and let her go again like a cat toying with a mouse, and she almost begged him, ''Okay, you win. Call management and get me thrown out, if you'd enjoy the sight of my humiliation. I won't bother to tell you why it matters so much. You'd only shrug.''

But he didn't make his first move, and in the end she didn't ask him to. Instead, she held desperately to the faint, fading hope that it would turn out all right. What other choice did she have?

Some minutes later, however, the Wainwrights came back, and despite Mrs. Wainwright's suspicious glare, her husband gallantly whirled Cat away to dance at last. Patrick, surprisingly, didn't interfere.

Suddenly, when she'd really believed all hope was lost, it was easy. Oh, it was so wonderfully easy! Here she was, out on the dance floor with a perspiring councillor, who was like putty in her hands.

One eager question from him about her ancestral home led her smoothly into the subject of chemical contamination of the poor, dear ancestral trout stream and consequent tragic demise of the poor, dear ancestral trout.

The councillor's open-jawed interest in everything she said then allowed her to run on about the charming bed-and-breakfast mansion she was staying at in upper Highgate Street, and how the owner of the bed-and-breakfast was very concerned about the proposed rezoning of one block of lower Highgate Street, where, she understood, the houses had been built on the sight of a former tannery.

The ground, according to the bed-and-breakfast owner, was hopelessly contaminated from the tanning chemicals below the surface of added top soil and rock fill, and it would be a tragedy, quite simply a shocking, frightful tragedy, if the contamination—not known about by the general public, by the way, because it had been hushed up—was brought to the surface through reckless bulldozing by developers.

In any case, the heritage value of the old Victorian houses on that particular block was, ''like my own ancestral estate of Dungrove Castle,'' absolutely priceless and must on no account be sacrificed to the frightful greed of commercial interests.

''Lady Catrina, you are absolutely right,'' said the councillor eagerly. ''You couldn't have known this, of course, but environmental contamination and deliberate hushing up of its presence is one of my most strongly felt issues, and it's the most amazing coincidence that I should meet someone like you who shares my concerns.''

He took a moment to mop his brow with a big, plaid handkerchief, as if the fluency of his oratory was exhausting him, then said, ''As for the heritage values, of course I wish we, here in the United States, had the sensitivity of you British nobles in that area. Rest assured, however, that this city—as well as you personally, my dear—''

He really did have a very pleasant smile, Cat noted.

"—can count on my influence in council to hold these forces of darkness at bay, and council is going to know that at the very next meeting, because I am not going to hold my cards to my chest any longer. The rezoning in lower Highgate Street is *off!*"

The music ended at that moment, and a very breathless Councillor Wainwright escorted Cat off the floor and back to the table.

Before he reached it, he was waylaid by his wife Darlene, saying urgently, "Earl? Earl! Grab that waitress. She's missed our table, and I'm ready for my supper. Those canapes wouldn't have fed a bird. Earl? Go *after* her!"

He loped off obediently in the wake of the waitress, almost forgetting about the ice in his eagerness. His wife, evidently not trusting either his persistence about supper or his immunity to any of the beautiful women here tonight, followed him.

Cat turned from the councillor and reached the table, her success glowing in her face and making her smile helplessly.

She'd done it. She had actually done it! Pixie's home and the other gracious Victorian houses in lower Highgate Street were safe, as were the other families who lived in them. Seven and a half weeks from now, when the vital council meeting was due to take place, sleazy Barry Grindlay would have no more reason to try and con poor, frail, simple-hearted Pixie out of her one and only asset.

Now, if she could only find Jill, tell her the good news and get out of here...

"Pleased about something, Lady Catrina?" said Patrick's darkly amused voice just a few feet away.

Cat dropped into her seat, knocked hollow by the man once more. Everyone else from this table was dancing or greeting friends, and he sat here alone. His long body was draped in his seat in a lazy sprawl and just one corner of his mouth was lifted in a smile.

Of course she hadn't forgotten about him. Somehow she suspected she wasn't going to find it very easy to do that, even after this event was over. His voice, his smile, the feel of his arms around her as they danced, his clever way with words and the searching, half-amused, half-cynical look in his blue eyes were all things that would haunt her, waking and sleeping, for weeks. And there was another quality to him, as well. Or maybe it was a quality in the air between them. Either way, she couldn't put a name to it.

But at least until a moment ago she had kidded herself that his involvement in her evening was done.

It was instantly apparent that he didn't agree. When she stammered out something inane about a frightfully pleasant conversation with Councillor Wainwright during the dance, he laughed aloud. It was a complicated sound, more than the simple expression of amusement.

"While there's no one else around," he suggested, leaning forward, "let's be a little more honest about this, shall we?"

"Wh-what do you mean?" she said, although she knew quite well.

"You have about as much right to call yourself

Lady Catrina Willoughby-Brown as I would have to call myself Prince Patrick of Kalamazoo," he answered. "Sorry, Lady C, but I've blown your cover. I know why you're really here, and I'm not going to let you get away with it...."

Chapter Three

"Unless," Patrick continued in a less threatening tone, "you agree to spend the next couple of hours with me."

The moment the words were out of his mouth, he regretted them. He'd already beaten off several ambitious young beauties while "Lady Catrina" was dancing with the councillor.

Beaten off. The expression fitted. They were like mosquitoes. Persistent and annoying, with buzzy little voices and blood-sucking intent. For a moment, the notion of spending time with a gold digger who hadn't targeted himself was appealing, but that moment soon passed.

To find her briefly fascinating was one thing. To open himself up to having her chase him was something very different.

Because if she was any good as a fortune hunter, she'd soon work out that he was a better target than Wainwright. He'd then have to endure the tedium,

and the disappointment of listening to her simper
and coo as she tried to draw his interest. Just another
mosquito....

"Don't," she begged, in answer to his impulsive
demand, and he was surprised out of his complacent
remorse when he heard the real anguish in her voice.

Also, for mercy's sake, what was happening to
those big brown eyes? Were those actually *tears*
making them glisten?

"Please don't," she went on, her voice shaky. "I
mean, I assume you're connected somehow with the
council or the zoning authority, or whoever, but...
but... Oh, damn, why am I begging?"

She dropped her head so that her mass of gorgeous hair fell forward like an avalanche of silk and
screened her emotion-filled face.

"As if begging is going to do any good!" she
muttered. "If you're serious about that bargain of
yours, of course I'll spend two hours with you. To
think you'd ruin or spare people's lives on the basis
of some faint interest in my company!"

"Actually, I'm viewing you more as a kind of
insect repellent," he drawled, masking his true reaction to her dramatically changed mood.

"Insect repellent?"

"Here comes another mosquito now."

"*Patrick!*" squealed Tiffany de Saint. "Patrick
Callahan! It's been a hundred *years!*"

She minced up to the table on impossible heels
and bent to kiss him, offering a deliberate glimpse
of breasts that had been professionally inflated to
more than generous size. When she straightened
again, Patrick noted that not a hair on her blond head
had moved, it was so stiffly styled.

He didn't know what favor she'd called in to get a ticket this evening, but she certainly wasn't here on the strength of service to charity, public profile or talent. He only knew her because she'd worked as the personal assistant to Anna Tarrant, a publicity consultant he'd dated for a while. She'd lost that job after sleeping with one too many of Anna's married clients.

Running into people like Tiffany was one of the things that made Patrick regret the litany of short-lived relationships with interesting women that formed his past. He now found that he knew too many people, and too many of those people he didn't like.

"Hi, Tiffany," he said. "Meet Lady Catrina Willoughby-Brown."

He slid an arm around Lady C's shoulders and saw Tiffany's face tighten. Her baby-blue eyes narrowed and went as hard as two diamonds above a rectangular smile that she couldn't sustain.

"*Lady* Catrina," she echoed. To her credit, she recognized defeat at once. "I'm just so utterly thrilled to meet you." Her voice was like damp cardboard. Seconds later, she had moved on.

"See," he said to Lady C. "Mosquito repellent."

"Yes, I see," she answered at once. "But if you think that makes it any better, I—I don't agree. Just because you have your own agenda. What are you doing? *Selling* your silence? It's…it's…just wrong!"

The phony accent had disappeared completely, replaced by pure, native Philadelphian, and either she hadn't even noticed or she didn't care anymore. It appalled Patrick to see how upset she was. Hell, she was shaking! He could see it and feel it, beneath the arm that he still had draped lightly across her shoulder.

"Hey!" he said urgently, straightening and taking his arm away. "Hey, Lady C!"

"Don't call me that."

"What should I call you then?"

"Just Cat, okay? No..." She shook her head, quickly changing her mind, and he saw the Wainwrights returning with their steaming supper plates. "Can you stick to Lady Catrina, please, as if you believed me? *Please!* Or else, if this means anything to you, five of us will lose our home."

"What?"

"Grindlay won't leave my cousin alone. He's trying to trick her into selling so that when the rezoning goes through he can get in first and develop the land. She's vulnerable and often gets confused. We can't ever trust that he won't find a way to get to her. This was the only thing we could think of, and now...I need the bathroom," she finished abruptly and hurried off before the Wainwrights reached the table.

Patrick sat back in his seat in stunned silence, his neck and face burning and his hands ice-cold.

What was that about? Sheesh! Who was talking about anyone losing their home? She had truly called his bluff just now, and she was too upset even to know it.

Clearly, he'd gotten something majorly wrong. She wasn't here, like Tiffany de Saint, to catch herself a rich boyfriend at all. She had targeted Earl P. Wainwright for another reason entirely. His mind made rapid, accurate leaps of logic. *Councillor* Wainwright. She'd talked about a rezoning…

The puzzle fell into place in a sketchy sort of way. She had used this ball to gain access to Wainwright and influence his vote on the local council over a zoning issue that affected her home, and evidently she was sure she'd succeeded after her dance with the affable councilman. Patrick remembered the sweet relief on Cat's face a few minutes ago when she'd returned to the table.

Without knowing the full story, he nevertheless approved. He knew a little about the workings of the local council in this particular obscure corner of Greater Philadelphia. In his opinion the council was way too fond of rezoning at the drop of a hat, making a mockery of sensitive city planning and development.

But the success of the plan, he calculated, had to depend on Wainwright continuing to fall for that British aristocrat thing, and this was why Lady C had been so upset to think of Patrick blowing her cover.

She'd fled to the bathroom to repair her makeup, while he was left feeling like a complete heel. He'd pictured her as a brazen gold digger, and he'd enjoyed the idea of exposing her. To him, it had been a bit of unusual entertainment for the evening, while clearly to her it was anything but.

Who was she? She had guts, imagination and flair, that was for sure, to attempt such a flamboyant scam. He was the only person who suspected she wasn't who she said she was, and that was only because—

Wham! The realization hit him in the guts.

It was only because from the moment he saw her he hadn't been able to take his eyes off her, hadn't been able to stop thinking about her. This had made him a witness to her occasional slips. And now that he understood her a little better, his interest was stronger than ever. He hadn't felt so immediately and totally fascinated by a woman for a very long time.

He sat there, toying with the rest of the food on his plate, impatient in every cell of his body for her to get back so he could learn more.

In the bathroom, Cat cooled her reddened eyes with wet tissue then set about patching up her makeup. She didn't do a good job, but maybe it didn't matter now. Maybe nothing mattered. She'd thought earlier that she had won the gamble of this saucy scheme, and instead she was hanging by a thread that Patrick Callahan could snip any time he chose.

And for some crazy reason—she didn't really buy the "mosquito repellent" thing; there was more to it than that—he was going to allow her companionship to buy his silence.

Just her companionship?

Oh, no. Uh-uh. Of course not!

It clicked.

The bargain Patrick Callahan undoubtedly had in mind was the one that would take place *after* the party. The one where she would sleep with him in return for his continued silence.

The CEO of Callahan Systems could probably get access to the private phone number of any city councilman in eastern Pennsylvania just by calling in one tiny favor. He could blow her story any time he liked. Would he do it just because she turned down the offer of his bed?

Cat calculated for a few minutes, her mind spinning. She had to decide if there was a warm, selfless human heart beating away somewhere in there beneath Patrick Callahan's good-looking exterior, with its aura of success and entitlement. And if there *was* such a heart, she had to appeal to it. She had to get him to care....

Maybe she's not coming back, Patrick started to wonder.

He shifted restlessly in his seat and tried not to crane his neck in the direction of the bathroom, looking for her. He had totally lost interest in the conversation at the table, lost interest in anything other than Lady C, and he knew that his brother Tom would be most disappointed in the schmoozing element of the evening.

As for the cruising...

Lauren Van Shuyler stopped by his table for a chat. She was an old friend. He'd done quite a bit of business with her father's company, and he genuinely liked her. But there was an inner sadness to her these days, and she'd never been a woman he could flirt with. A couple more women made their interest evident, in a similar style to Tiffany de Saint, but for some reason the very idea of even talking with them...let alone dancing, flirting, taking them home...wearied him beyond belief.

''Hello...''

His head shot up. It was Cat, smiling halfheartedly down at him. No, Lady Catrina, he corrected himself. He owed it to her to think of her that way. She was back from the bathroom, and he had been so busy brooding on the probability that she'd left the ball altogether that he hadn't even noticed.

"Hi," he said carefully.

She slipped into the seat beside him, her tentative smile still in place. "I hope I wasn't gone too long."

"Well, I did think about sending out a search party," he drawled.

"I'm sorry."

"Hey…" He frowned. Something was different. She had her chin held high, and she had "Lady Catrina" patchily in place, but she looked scared, and her sugar-brown eyes were full of uncertainty.

Wainwright and his wife were dancing again, and no one else at this large table had a starry-eyed fascination with the British aristocracy, so they weren't taking much notice of either him or Lady C.

Patrick said to her quickly, "Let's dance. I'm afraid you missed dessert."

"I don't care. Dancing's fine."

She got up obediently, almost timidly, and again he wondered, "What's happened?" Then he found that he'd said it aloud.

"I—I don't know what you mean," she stammered, accent back in place.

They didn't wait for the escorts over the ice. Instead, he just grabbed her, and they skittered across to the dance floor. He could feel the tension making every muscle in her body brittle and hard.

"You're acting different," he said when they reached the dance floor. "At first, earlier tonight, you couldn't stand me." He grinned. "And I kind of liked that."

"Sure you did!" She raised one eyebrow.

"I did," he insisted. "It was...an experience I haven't had very often."

"Uh-huh," she nodded slowly, understanding. "It would be, I guess."

"You're not slow on the uptake, are you?"

"Not generally."

"Then you got upset," he said, continuing his recap of the shifting balances between them. "And, Cat..."

"Lady Catrina," she reminded him.

"Lady Catrina," he parroted obediently, "I'm *so* sorry I rattled you like that. You have to believe that!" He took both her hands and squeezed them, brought them up to chest level and clasped them inside his palms.

"Are you?" She narrowed her eyes and searched his face, as though gauging the depth of his sincerity was really important to her.

It was, he realized. Of course it was!

"Oh, good grief, I know what it is!" he said, looking down at her. "You think if you're not...nice to me now, then I'll call security, or something. And if you're not even nicer to me later, I'll have a tiny little word in Wainwright's ear and waste all of your careful planning."

"And you're telling me you won't? Puh-lease! Try and make it convincing!" Suddenly, all the spirit and fire and determination was back. She pulled away from him and Patrick felt the hairs on his neck stand on end. Damn, but she had courage! Class, too.

"Of course I'm telling you I won't!" he said. "Hell, what kind of a man do you think I am?"

"A rich one."

He didn't even dignify the cynical interjection with a reply and went on as if he hadn't heard her, "Do you really think I need to resort to cheap blackmail to get a woman into bed?"

"Some men would find that amusing, whether they needed to or not," she answered coolly.

With her pride back in place, she wasn't going to give him an inch. Which was brave of her, considering what she thought he might do to her plan.

"Well, Lady C, believe me, I can find a lot better ways to amuse myself than that," he told her, his voice rising in his effort to get through to her.

And, damn it, he was going to get through to her! he vowed, not stopping for a second to consider why it was so important.

He gripped her by the shoulders, rounding his hands softly over those warm, smooth knobs of muscle. Then he looked into her eyes as if he could hypnotize her into trusting him. All around them, dancers gyrated or spun, and colored lights swathed the darkness with their dazzling beams.

"Catrina—and will you please damn well let me leave off the Lady!—you have to trust me!"

"Why?" she demanded simply.

"Because—because you have no choice, my lady," he repeated, now with total confidence. He could see the logic of it in his head like a game of chess. "Either I'm a complete scum who'll blow your cover to Wainwright because you won't sleep with me tonight." The wicked part of him made him add, "By the way, I'm right in that, aren't I? You won't sleep with me tonight?"

"Not on your life!"

"Good," he drawled, "Because, as it happens, I'm not asking."

He fixed her with such a steady glare that she had to know he meant it. Intimacy with a stranger at the end of a long and very superficial evening had lost its appeal for him quite a while ago.

"Ah," she said.

"Clear?"

"Yes." Her color was high.

He picked up the logic of his argument again. "Or I'm *not* a complete scum, and you're safe. Either way, you have no choice. No influence. You can't sweet-talk a scum out of behaving like one, and if I'm not one, then you don't need to."

"Sweet-talk?"

"Sweet-talk," he confirmed. "That's what you were trying to do a minute ago, isn't it?"

"Uh, yes, I guess it was." Her eyes narrowed again, and she studied him with her head tilted just a little to one side, as if she still didn't know what to make of any of this.

"So just be yourself," he ordered, then added a belated and not particularly patient, "Please!"

"Myself," Cat repeated slowly.

"With small but essential overtones of Lady Catrina, of course," Patrick Callahan reassured her seriously.

All at once a bubble of laughter escaped from Cat's lips. "You make her sound like a type of fragrance."

"She is. Very prim and old-fashioned, like English lavender."

"That's not what I'm wearing."

"What are you wearing, then?" He bent his head

and breathed in the fragrance of her soft cloud of hair, glad of the excuse. He'd wanted to do this for, oh, at least an hour. "Not a whole lot," he said, answering his own question. Her hair tickled his nose and he wanted to bury his face in it.

"Shampoo," she confirmed.

"Just?"

"Soap, too, I guess. I knew any fragrance we could afford would have smelled cheap and spoiled the illusion."

"We?"

"Yes. We," Cat said, then closed her lips, determined not to open up any further. That could get dangerous. She'd already said far too much to him. He didn't need to hear about her sisters, her nephew, and Pixie.

He was still for a moment. She could see him weighing up the issue. Ask more questions, or leave her alone? When he simply shrugged, she knew he'd made his decision. No more questions. The tension left her body on a shuddering sigh.

"Shh, it's okay, Lady C," he soothed her softly, taking her hands in his again and rubbing the backs of them gently with the balls of his thumbs. "Honest, it's completely okay."

Then he drew her closer and they danced.

Oh, did they dance! They admitted to each other, after some minutes and a change of tempo in the music, that they didn't know a whole lot of steps beyond that waltz he'd been so good at earlier. This meant there was only one choice. They had to hold each other and sway and turn. Their bodies had to melt more closely together with every movement, until her hand rested on his shoulder and his cheek rested on her hair.

Cat could feel him, his warmth and his breathing, and smell him, musky and male, with a hint of pine and sweet Mirabeau wine. Her dress tangled in his legs, and even through the layers of silver underskirt, she could feel their warmth and strength. She could have turned her face upward and brushed her lips across his, and she had a sweet, beguiling certainty that the touch of his mouth would feel and taste completely fabulous.

She didn't emerge from this strange trance of sensation until Jill glided past, carrying a tray piled dangerously with dirty glasses. Jill somehow managed to catch Cat's eye, frown and tap her left wrist with one finger.

Cat gasped. Oh-my-lord! The time!

Without thinking, she grabbed Patrick's wrist, which was warm and solid and covered lightly in dark hair. He wore a watch, which she dimly registered was Swiss and made of two colors of gold.

But what really struck her was the position of the gold hands. Much later than she would have thought, and she had to work tonight. Her friend Jackie, who also worked at the child-care center, was covering for her until after the ball, but then Jackie wanted to go home and get a good night's sleep, and Cat had promised to take over for the last half of her shift.

"Jackie's going to kill me!" she said aloud, and backed out of Patrick's arms. "I'm sorry…. Good night, Patrick. I have to go."

She could have and should have left…oh, long ago.

Her purse was still at the table. She teetered across the ice, seized the black satin purse strap, and managed a gushing and aristocratic goodbye to Councillor Wainwright, who looked as if he was getting ready to leave also. Then she fled, and didn't realize—though perhaps she should have done—that Patrick was following her.

She was already through the ice-rink doors and into the entrance lobby when she heard his voice just behind her.

"Wait, Cat!"

"No, I'm sorry, Patrick, I'm late. It was…fun. And thanks for, you know, not—for understanding that this was—"

She didn't take the time to finish, just pushed open the outer door and went out into the humid June night.

But he was still behind her.

"Listen, stop! You can't just leave like this, when we've—when I have no idea who you really are."

"It's not important."

"Isn't it?" he demanded. Twin threads of arrogance and eagerness twisted together in his voice.

"N-no!" She found it surprisingly hard to make the word come out.

"It *is*," he insisted. "We had a great time tonight. It was—I don't know. It meant something. We—"

Cat didn't listen. Not that it was easy just to leave like this. Her skin was still alive and hot from the way they'd touched. But she had no illusions about what Patrick Callahan had felt, even if he did.

Skittering down the cement steps outside the rink, she felt her spike-heeled shoe come loose. She had bought the black velvet pumps from a charity store and they were a size too big. In fact, there were blisters on her heels, she realized in some surprise. They hurt. Why hadn't she felt them before?

Deliberately, she kicked the shoe right off and left it on the step. Patrick could have it, if he liked. A little memento of the evening.

Like Cinderella.

Then, reaching the flat sidewalk, she bent down, pulled off the other one and threw it over her shoulder. No sense doing things by halves. It was a lot quicker to run barefoot.

She lifted her dress and sprinted, the silvery underskirts frothing around her legs. She wasn't as fit or agile as Jill, but she did her share of running in the park with Jill's little Sam a couple of times a week, and she didn't have far to go tonight.

Patrick had stopped on the steps. Cat turned her head for a fraction of a second. Good grief, he'd picked up the shoe!

She didn't wait to see what he'd do next, just darted across the road. A car swished by, cutting between her and Patrick. She sprinted again, till she got around the corner, keys in hand, and gained the safety of Pixie's classic orange Volkswagen Beetle, which she'd had to borrow this evening as the ancient and decrepit Buick she shared with her stepsisters had flat-out refused to perform today.

Then she sat at the wheel for a moment, breathing heavily and not at all sure whether she should laugh or cry. Why on earth was she feeling so emotional, suddenly? The evening was over. She had what she wanted. Pixie's house was safe, and that was all that mattered.

It *was* all that mattered! She laughed aloud, gulped back a dizzy sob, and started the engine.

Chapter Four

"This," Patrick said to himself aloud, "is completely ridiculous!"

He had given up his pursuit of her at the top of the steps. Now he stood there, feeling more helpless than he remembered feeling in his entire life. In his hand, there was a size-nine black velvet shoe, property of someone who called herself Lady Catrina Willoughby-Brown, and in his ears there was a ringing sound, origin unknown.

"I am *not* standing here, at three minutes after midnight, on the steps of a suburban ice rink with a shoe in my hand...."

There was a tinny little roar as a car came around the corner and zipped along the street just in front of him. An orange car. Shaped kind of like a pumpkin. With a barefoot mystery woman at the wheel.

"...and I am *not* watching a pumpkin-colored Volkswagen Beetle disappearing into the night, driven by a woman whose real name I don't even know, and wondering how I'm going to find her again.''

But denial was ineffective on this occasion. He had to embrace the horrible truth. Not only was he suddenly living in a fairy tale, but for the first time in his life, he actually, wholeheartedly believed in them.

He had Cinderella's shoe in his hand. Its match was staring saucily at him from the sidewalk several feet away. And he knew at once without even thinking about it that he was going to embrace his destiny, take action and somehow find the woman.

Purely to give her her shoes back, of course.

He went down the steps and picked up the second shoe. Weighing both of them in his hand, he decided in a dazed sort of way that they were far too big. *This* Cinderella didn't have dainty feet, for sure! Then he wandered across to the parking lot to reclaim his car. He had spent so little time on wooing Wainwright and his companions on the issue of software purchases from Callahan Systems that none of them seemed remotely interested. Tom and Connor would be disappointed, but Patrick couldn't find it in himself to care at the moment.

''She's a dream, sir. She's totally, totally a dream!'' the young valet parking attendant said fervently, handing Patrick the keys to his late-model Porsche C4 Cabriolet.

''No,'' he answered vaguely. ''She's real. I think. I mean, I spent practically the whole evening with her. She has to be real. The question is…''

He blinked and focused, caught the look of total confusion on the parking attendant's face and realized, oh my lord, he's talking about the damned car!

"Thanks. Glad you enjoyed driving, uh, *her*," he managed, and arrived home thirty-five minutes later without the slightest memory of how he'd gotten there.

The next day, it was only his fairy-tale role model that kept him mentally afloat. What had Prince Charming said? "I shall not rest until I find she whose foot this slipper fits."

Or words to that effect.

Okay, great. He had a clear-cut, goal-oriented strategy. He was accustomed to that, and it felt good.

The prince had adopted a simple approach of search and elimination, but it was hardly practical in this case. Patrick didn't have a retinue of under-employed footmen wearing white curly wigs at his disposal, and he suspected that the greater Philadelphia area in the twenty-first century was rather more heavily populated with size-nine female feet than Fairyland had been five hundred years ago. He would have to apply brain power.

No, he would have to get therapy....

Fact one. She probably lived pretty locally, and she didn't have a lot of money. He quickly decided that fact one was a dead end.

Fact two...

No, not fact, intuition. He suddenly put a couple of things together and realized, "She knows the ice rink. What was it she said when we were talking about the decor? That it "usually" looked so bland? She's been there before. Often. And there's the issue of the invitation. Those were pretty exclusive, and they checked them at the door. Getting hold of one must have been an inside job. She works there, or

she knows someone who does. I've cracked it! I can
trace her through the ice rink!''

Yes, definitely. Serious therapy. Soon.

No, *soon* was when he was going to front up at
the rink. Like, first thing Monday morning, in his
most intimidating and expensive business suit, with
the aura of a man who is used to having his questions answered.

''I, uh, found these shoes.''

Holding them out like a peace offering and wondering why he sounded like a guilty five-year-old in
a school playground, Patrick registered the startled
widening of the young woman's eyes.

''Uh, at the Mirabeau Ball?'' she said.

''Yes.''

They were both standing in the chilly and spa-
cious ice-rink ticket office. It was eight-thirty in the
morning, and there was a faint mist hovering over
the scratched and scoured surface of the ice. Saturday night's glamorous decor had disappeared. Serious skaters wearing practice clothes and expensive
skates looped and zoomed around. There came the
sounds of blades clashing or gouging into the ice,
and every couple of minutes a piece of rather tinny
music started up on the distorting sound system.

A skinny teenage girl appeared at the ticket window. ''Hi, Jill. Can I have a new monthly pass,
please?''

''Could you, um, please excuse me for a moment?'' the young woman—Jill—asked Patrick with
an edgy-looking smile.

''Yeah, go right ahead,'' he invited, and watched
her take the girl's money and issue the pass.

He thought he recognized Jill. Hadn't she been one of the skating waitresses here on Saturday night? It made sense. What might also turn out to make sense was her uneasiness. She had recognized those shoes, he was sure of it.

When she had finished helping the girl, she turned back to him. She'd had time to prepare her story, now.

"Okay, thanks for dropping them in," she said much more smoothly. "I'll put up a notice so someone can claim them. Thanks," she repeated.

Keen to get rid of him?

Testing this suspicion, Patrick lingered, stalling. "But what if they don't belong to someone who comes to the rink?" he said. "The vast majority of the guests at Saturday's ball don't, I imagine."

Now she was definitely nervous. "I guess not," she said. "But, you know, someone might call, or something. I—"

She stopped and he turned, following the arrow-straight direction of her gaze.

And there she was. Cinderella herself. He couldn't believe it was so easy.

"Hi, Jill," she said, shouldering the door closed behind her. "I brought some Danish and coffee. Did you want me to pick up—?"

When she caught sight of Patrick, Cat stopped dead. Didn't say another word. The three of them just stood there.

Patrick was the first one to find his voice, but it didn't come out as it normally did. Instead it was husky, uncertain. What was happening to him?

"You left your shoes behind when the clock struck midnight, Cinderella," he said to her.

There was a tiny beat of silence, then, "They hurt," she answered.

The phone buzzed, taking Jill out of the equation, which Patrick was thankful for. Jill was bristling, as if she knew all about Patrick, every last sorry detail, and wasn't impressed.

"Do you always leave your shoes behind when they hurt?" he asked.

"I got them from a charity store. They only cost three dollars."

"Three-dollar shoes to the biggest event on Philadelphia's social calendar this summer?"

"Yeah, well, I didn't pay for my ticket, so it seemed appropriate. A no-frills evening all round."

"Except for the beautiful ball-dress, Cinders."

"I have access to a fairy godmother. She did the dress for free."

She put down the coffee and the Danish, folded her arms and looked at him, chin raised. Color began to seep into her cheeks, and her eyes looked darker than usual. Patrick could sense the pull between them, even stronger than it had been the other night. Was it the honesty of daylight?

A part of him had expected to find that the spell was broken, but instead the magic was woven more powerfully, and she felt it, too. He knew she did.

"Your friend Jill here got the ticket for you, right?" he asked.

"My stepsister Jill, actually, but yes." Catrina confirmed. Then something made her add, "The whole thing was her idea."

Back in March, in Las Vegas, Jill had taken part in something called a "Cinderella Marriage Marathon" and this had somehow convinced her of the deep relevance of fairy tales in modern life. All of a sudden Catrina felt that she understood what Jill meant...

Catrina looked very different today, Patrick decided. She was tired around the eyes, as if she hadn't slept, but she was energized, as if she'd already been on the go for a couple of hours. Her face was bare of makeup so that it looked smooth, a little shiny and incredibly fresh and open.

She was casually dressed in calf-length black pants, a powder blue tank top with an edging of cotton lace and a thin little cardigan of the same lace-edged cotton knit over the top. The fabric hugged the smooth knobs of her shoulders and stretched snugly across her high breasts. She had her hair in two braids just behind her ears. Like a Swiss milkmaid, or something. It shouldn't have suited her, but it did.

Jill was off the phone again. "You two want to use the rink manager's private office?" she offered, as if she could sense what was going on. "Gina doesn't get here until nine."

"Thanks, but we're going to go for coffee," Patrick said.

"No, we're not," Catrina answered him back, in a heartbeat.

Patrick spread his hands helplessly. "Aren't we? Why not? Is a simple cup of coffee such a major threat?"

Jill opened the manager's office and motioned them both inside with exaggerated politeness.

"Please," she said. "Have some privacy. But you know what I think, Cat."

So her name really was Catrina? Cat for short. He liked it.

"Yes, I do. And I agree with you," Cat said to her sister. The door shut with a pointed action from Jill, leaving Cat and Patrick alone. "Which is why I'm not going for coffee with you, Patrick Callahan," she finished.

Catrina was still slightly weak in the legs from the shock of seeing him here with Jill a couple of minutes ago. She and her stepsister had talked about it yesterday. Oh boy, had they talked about it! Suzanne had been working at the library and Pixie had taken Sam to a church function, so Jill and Cat had been alone in Pixie's big, slightly run-down old house.

"What was the deal with the guy you were dancing with?" Jill had wanted to know. "Did he have anything to do with convincing Councillor Wainwright?"

"No, he was just a distraction," Cat had blurted out.

"Some distraction! At one stage, there, just before you left, it was difficult to tell where he began and you left off!"

"I know." Cat had made a face. "But I'll never see him again, so a bit of... I don't know. What was it? Flirting, I guess...couldn't do any harm. Anyway, he wasn't my type."

"What, rich and soulless?"

"Exactly! I don't have to tell you, do I?"

"Since a man like that ruined my life? No!"

"Did he really ruin your life, Jill? I mean, you love your little guy."

"True," Jill had said, her face softening. "I'm

crazy about Sam, and I'd never in a million years wish he hadn't been born. But getting pregnant and having Curtis Harrington turn his Ivy-League back on me the moment he found out about it wasn't fun at first. It got us kicked out of Mom's, didn't it? Had us all living in a trailer park for four years?''

''We don't live in a trailer park anymore.''

''No, we got lucky,'' Jill had admitted. ''My mom dumped all those old boxes of your dad's stuff on you one day, and there were those old letters between your mom and Pixie, when you didn't even know your mom had a cousin. So now we live in a Victorian mansion with a sagging porch, which twice a week we have to stop Pixie from giving away to that con man Grindlay. We share the crummiest car in the world, and college is taking you a lo-o-ng time, around the full-time job you have to work. As Mom would say—if she still spoke to us— we've ''found our level.'' And I don't think men like Curtis Harrington III—or your guy last night— get serious about gals in that situation, either.''

''Neither do I,'' Cat had agreed, before adding, ''But fortunately, since I'm never going to see Patrick Callahan again, and never *want* to see Patrick Callahan again, it's not an issue.''

Only now here he was. With an agenda.

''Is coffee such a big deal?'' he repeated.

He seemed totally in control, cool, intelligent and achingly good-looking in his dark business suit. He was leaning one hand on the manager's desk and looking up at her through long black lashes.

''No, coffee's not a big deal,'' she agreed with an outward calm that she didn't fully feel inside. ''But you've got to ask yourself why you're doing this, Patrick."

"*I* have to ask myself?"

"Yes, because I already know."

She lifted her chin and faced him straight on, aware of the power of her attraction to him but immune from it now, with Jill's words, and her own, fresh in her mind. The fact that she was tired after a busy and sleepless night at the child-care center helped, too. Patrick Callahan could have no idea about working all night for not a lot more than minimum wage, so that she'd have a hope of a decent career in a decent profession some day.

"You were curious about me the other night," she told him. "I was just a little bit different, wasn't I?"

"More than a little bit, Cinderella."

"You wanted to know where I was coming from with all that Lady Catrina stuff. Then you found out. Like you said just now, I was Cinderella that night, conning her way into the ball. And you've gotten a bit of a kick out of playing the role of the prince."

"*I* got a kick? Are you telling me that letting your shoe drop like that was an accident?"

"Guilty as charged," she answered him. "I could have gone back for it. I guess I wanted to leave something behind. But that's irrelevant. What counts is the real life ending to that sweet Cinderella tale. You know it, Patrick!"

"Do I?"

"That Charming guy was never really serious about Cinderella," she said. "He just got her pregnant in the palace garden, then dumped her cold and married the princess next door. Happened to Jill.

And as my stepmother would say, people find their level.''

"Are you saying—?''

"I'm saying, think about it and be honest with yourself,'' she insisted. "You were looking for something a little bit different, and for one night I was it. But that's all it was. And I *am* different. I'm not from your world.''

Quickly, she sketched in her background.

"I got kicked out of home by my stepmother, along with my two stepsisters—''

"Stepsisters, too, huh, Cinders? Jill and—?''

She ignored him, "—when Jill and I were both eighteen. My dad—I loved my dad—who Rose never stopped telling us to his face that she 'never should have married...' Well, he'd died a year before that, and he didn't leave much. What he did leave, through an oversight on his part, went to Rose. For four years we lived in a trailer park in a part of this city you've never even seen. Now we share most of a big old house in lower Highgate Street, with my sweet, elderly cousin who's not fit to work anymore, who can't manage her budget, and who'd be out on the streets if it wasn't for us. None of us have two pennies to rub together by the time each payday rolls around.''

"Okay...''

"I'm trying to study, and that's my goal, just to drag myself over a couple more hurdles and get my nursing degree. That's a pretty tame ambition for someone from your side of the tracks. You don't want what I want, and I don't want you.''

Ah, shoot, why was she crying about it? She had

done so well until now. Cat dabbed quickly at her eyes with the sleeve of her cardigan.

But she could see that Patrick had seen the tears, and they had made him freeze. His face was set, thoughtful and quite shocked, as if a woman who could speak so bluntly was a species of creature he hadn't encountered before. As for the tears, he probably thought they were faked. After all, she had proved to him on Saturday night how adept she was at faking things.

He spoke at last. He hadn't tried to come any closer. He wasn't tempted to kiss away her tears, evidently. But he'd straightened from the desk.

"Uh, in view of your cogent presentation of your case," he said, his voice still husky, "I think it would be wise if I retracted my offer of coffee."

"Yeah, I think so, too, Patrick," she answered with a tired sigh.

It was hard to say the words, but she meant them, and she wasn't surprised when he wheeled around and left the rink manager's office without a fight.

Out in the street as he strode to his car, Patrick felt as if he'd been slugged in the guts by a fast-pitched baseball. Her refusal was the last thing he'd expected. The glass bubble of the fairy tale he'd been living in since Saturday night shattered, and he cursed himself.

For his arrogance. For his lack of perception. For the naively romantic heart that still beat away inside him, despite years of carefully cultivated cynicism.

Because, damn it, she was right. What did he really want from this, in the glaring light of day? What could he possibly want, if not some short-lived, mildly amusing affair? Nothing else made any sense.

As she'd said, they were from different worlds, and they were going in different directions.

He ought to do exactly as she had said. Turn around, get serious about his future and marry someone like sad-eyed Lauren Van Shuyler, the princess next door.

So why did the idea send such a chill desolation over his spirits, even as the first seed of rebellion began to sprout inside him? He didn't like being consigned to a stereotype. He didn't like being proved wrong. And he didn't particularly like losing his battles.

The only question that remained was what he planned to do about it.

Chapter Five

"I've got to stop doing this!" Patrick muttered to himself.

It was only the second time he'd cruised slowly down Catrina Brown's street in the ten days since the ball, but that was two times too often. Was he turning into a stalker? A voyeur?

Not a very successful one, if that was the case. He hadn't set eyes on her. Yet his struggle to either a) forget the woman or b) come up with a strategy for getting her interested was proving a dismal failure.

He just wasn't used to this! He'd learned certain things about life in thirty-six years of living it—and living it, he had to say, with a healthy degree of success.

First, if you wanted something, you went after it. You applied thought and effort and strategy. You believed in yourself. You believed in your goal. You didn't fall at the first hurdle. Second, you definitely didn't take notice of other people's dire predictions of failure. Other people frequently had no imagination, no access to your vision.

Approaching life according to these tenets, he and his younger brother Tom now found themselves at the head of a hugely successful software company, and Patrick had no reason to think that the same approach would yield less gratifying results in the personal sphere.

On the contrary.

Face to face with Cinder...er...Catrina in her day-to-day guise, he had at first accepted her poignantly cynical take on the ancient fairy tale. From the moment he'd left the ice rink, however, he'd begun to rebel.

"Since when did I take any notice of that wrongside-of-the-tracks nonsense?" he muttered to himself now, nosing the customized sapphire-blue Porsche slowly down the shade-filled street.

A big piece of Victorian red brick mansion hove into view. He wasn't totally sure that this was Cat's house, but the odds were good. It was in the right block of Highgate Street, the one that was set for rezoning. There was a mixture of shabbiness and cheerfulness about the place that fitted what he knew about Catrina and her unconventional family, also.

The porch was sagging and thick with a green vine at one corner. The gutters were rusted. The paint was peeling. There were some broken slates on the roof. The grass had apparently been mowed with a pair of blunt nail scissors.

But that same sagging porch was crowded with red geraniums in a higgledy-piggledy assortment of pretty containers, and there was an ancient swing-

and-slide set planted on that shaggy lawn at the side of the house, spruced up with new chains and fresh paint.

As he passed the house, he got another clue that he'd picked the right place. A small boy—stepsister Jill's son?—came out the side door, followed by an elderly woman—that cousin with the unlikely name of Pixie? They each carried a jar of bubble mix and a little plastic wand, and chains of glistening bubbles were already streaming into the warm summer air.

It was a quarter of twelve. Time for a nice half hour of bubble-blowing before lunch.

Ah, yes, lunch...

Patrick had teased himself with the idea that he would simply pass Cat in the street, flag her down and suggest burgers or a picnic. He'd *never* taken any notice of that wrong-side-of-the-tracks nonsense! Sheesh! He could instantly name at least a dozen qualities that were far more important to him than background and bank balance.

Like, say...as the side door opened again and Cat herself came out, blowing bubbles with a wand and a jar as well...the ability to grow red geraniums and the tendency to keep several jars of bubble mix on hand in the house.

Patrick's foot hovered over the accelerator pedal. He lifted it an inch...and then squeezed it down, putting speed into his vehicle and noise into the quiet street. He passed the house and lost sight of Cat and her family.

Of course he could have turned back, stopped the car, parked and said hello. But he didn't.

Why?

Because somehow he knew the look that would

appear on her face when she turned from her bubbles and saw him. Wary, skeptical, full of fight and contrariness, and most definitely not pleased to see him.

If it hadn't been for the bubbles, maybe he could have dealt with that look. If he'd interrupted her in hacking away at that hopeless lawn or collecting a wad of unwanted junk mail from the box that was wired precariously to a pillar on the porch.

But *bubbles?* To see her looking daggers at him through a cloud of *bubbles?*

No. This was about strategy, he reminded himself. He was going to pick his moment better than that.

Four days later, Patrick had grumpily convinced himself that he wasn't going to pick his moment with Catrina Brown at all.

Why put himself through that grief for a woman he hardly knew? What, exactly, had he felt about her, anyway? A stubborn need to prove himself as sensitive and open-minded about her background as the next man? Was that a good reason?

He distrusted himself. Distrusted everything about his reactions at the moment. What was happening, here? It was the night of July fourth. He'd had three different invitations from friends and family to go eat barbecue and watch fireworks, and he'd turned every one of them down. The only one he had been remotely tempted to accept was his old friend Lauren's. And that, he suspected, was only because he sensed the kinship between her aura of vague sadness and distance and his own mood at the moment.

But Lauren's dad was going to be there, and he would no doubt try to matchmake as he'd been doing for several years. Lauren would apologize for it at frequent intervals because she was even less interested in the idea than Patrick, and the whole thing would be awkward.

Just as awkward as a night of family with mom and dad and assorted brothers. Just as awkward as several hours of hot, unwanted sex...or, more likely, of strenuously avoiding hot, unwanted sex...with Abigail Wakefield.

Ah, hell!

Instead, he ate pizza alone in front of his embarrassingly huge television, then got in his car and drove through the exploding, smoke-filled night, mulling over the professional issue that plagued him at the moment.

Tom and Connor wanted him to set up an office of Callahan Systems in New York. He was the one with the most portable life. He was...or had become...the company schmoozer. The move made sense. So why was he reluctant? Was it simply his stubbornness again? The same stubbornness that wouldn't let him admit defeat over his inconvenient attraction to Catrina Brown?

Catrina Brown... Ah, hell! Again! She just wouldn't disappear, and for some reason that street sign just ahead read Highgate Street, and he was thinking about her yet again.

"What am I looking for this time?" he said to himself aloud, in utter disgust.

The street was deserted. With pink and green stars lighting the sky above the trees further ahead, filling the air with their dry, percussive popping, it seemed darker than usual, too. The park was not far distant, and cars belonging to dozens of spectators lined the curbs on both sides.

There was even a small, nondescript red vehicle double-parked two houses down, and Patrick's attention was caught by a darkly garbed figure loping toward it, slamming the door and gunning the engine down the street just ahead of him.

Strange.

He hadn't locked his focus onto the figure soon enough, but he could have sworn it had come from Cat's house. Was this an observed fact? Or evidence of his persistent interest? Some might call it an obsession. Everything seemed to come back to Catrina Brown at the moment.

The car was already out of sight around the next corner, and he had the last three numbers of its license plate taking up valuable space in his mind. This was partly because he was curious about where the figure had come from and partly because the numbers happened to reflect his birthday. 310. March the tenth.

Dismissing the subject for the moment, Patrick reached the bottom of the street, heard the final crescendo of the fireworks display begin, made a decision and turned again.

Okay. Enough of this. Enough.

He'd head over to mom and dad's, where he might just be in time to help load a couple of sleepy little nieces into their carseats, then share a late supper with his parents. He would probably get roped into scraping plates and stacking dishes. Fine by him. It was about time he did something useful for the people who mattered in his life, instead of chasing rainbows.

Rainbows who weren't interested.

But something was happening at Cat's house. This time he didn't stop to curse himself for glancing instinctively toward the place yet again. There was a flickering glow spilling through the bevelled glass panels in the front door, and it wasn't a reflection of the fireworks.

It was fire.

There was no place to park. He swung into the first empty driveway he could find, then ran back, horrified to see how much the blaze had advanced even in so short a time. As if something had helped it along.

Cell phone in hand, he called 911 and gave the details, stopping short at the dispatcher's questions.

"How many occupants are in the house, sir? Is anyone trapped?"

"I don't know."

Hell, I don't know. Are they all at the fireworks? he wondered, his brain shrieking stridently.

Then, behind him, he heard the protesting scrape of a wooden window sash being raised at the side of the house and yelled into the phone, "Yes! There's at least one person in the house. You gotta get the fire truck here damned fast!"

Because smoke was pouring out the window, surrounding the figure, masking it and choking it. Was it Cat? Jill?

No, the elderly cousin, Pixie. Struggling to see through the smoke, he recognized plump, papery arms that couldn't have belonged to Cat, her sisters or the child. Pixie was whimpering and yelling in a panic, and he couldn't make out a word. What was she doing? Were those pillows she was flinging to the ground? Why?

She disappeared and came back a moment later, and more pillows appeared out of the dark yellow-brown smoke. It looked poisonous.

This time, he managed to call to her, sizing up the situation better than she could in her fear.

"Not that way!" he yelled. "The front room, over the porch. There's an open window." Through which more smoke was pouring. He could hear smoke alarms screaming electronically inside the house. "You can slide down. I can catch you. It isn't so far to the ground from there."

"No, I can't! My dog! My dog!"

"Throw your dog down to me. You have to *hurry!*"

The smoke was getting thicker and darker, oily and toxic from burning wood varnish and paint. Patrick calculated that it must be the main staircase that was on fire, at the very center of the house. If Pixie didn't jump soon...

"I have her!"

The frail, shrill, frightened voice drew his attention back to the window, and he saw her holding out a tiny dog who was yapping and writhing in fear. He lunged into position as she hurled the animal wildly with no warning, so that he had to lunge again far to the left in order to catch the little creature. He did it awkwardly, and there was a yelp of pain.

"I'm sorry, puppy," he said. "I've got no time to see if you're hurt."

"Here, I'll take her!" said a voice beside him. He

looked sideways to see another elderly woman. "I'm a neighbor."

There were one or two other neighbors now, people who hadn't bothered with the fireworks, converging on the house.

"Great. Great," he answered the woman automatically.

He pushed the little dog quickly into her arms, where it panted and trembled and yapped despite her efforts to soothe it. Up in the smoke-screened window, there was no sign of Pixie. He yelled. Waited a second or two. Yelled again. Then didn't wait any longer.

How strong was that wisteria vine, doing its best to pull down one corner of the front porch? For that matter, how strong was the porch?

Strong enough. He climbed up. One foot gave way on a knot of woody vine but he shifted his weight and reached the gutter safely. Hauling himself onto the porch roof, he heard it creak, heard the roar of the fire, heard sirens in the distance, the voices of the fireworks spectators beginning to stream along the street now that the display was over, and the sound of their car doors banging as they reached their vehicles.

He took no notice of any of this. The ridged lip of the gutter pressed painfully into his groin as he rolled onto the roof, then he crab-walked up the steep pitch to the window, punched in the screen and dove through.

His hand landed on Pixie's shoulder, and she was lucky it hadn't been the whole weight of his body. Dressed in a floral housecoat with her fluffy gray

hair in pincurls, she was sprawled on the floor, over-
come by the smoke.

He yelled at her, "Is there anyone else in the
house? Damn it, is there anyone else in the house?"

Crazy. How could she answer when she was un-
conscious?

There was no time to think about how to do this.
He shouldered her weight, kind of *pitched* her, almost. She went out of the window head-first, with
his arms wrapped around her thighs to drag her back
just enough so she didn't bump her head. Then he
followed her in a clumsy lunge.

Hell, it was a pretty unprofessional rescue, no
points at all for elegance, but he didn't care. It
worked, and they slid down the porch roof with an
uncontrolled and painful clatter, saved only by the
wisteria. It snared them both in its nest of cool green
leaves.

The fire department was here, with police and am-
bulances in its wake. Seconds later, both he and
Pixie were on the ground, and the ambulance crew
zeroed in on the elderly woman with oxygen equipment and an IV and temporary protective dressings
for burns. A second crew tried to attach itself to
Patrick, but though he was choking and wheezing,
with his heart going like a train, he fought them off.

"There may be more people in the house, but I
don't know," he yelled, the smoke in his lungs cutting like knives, threatening to block his breathing.
"There's three more women that live here, and a
little boy. I don't know if they were at home tonight.
We've got to go back in there. We can't take the
chance."

And then he heard Cat's voice, a high, strident

shriek cutting instantly through all the other noise around him, cutting straight to his heart. "Oh, sweet heaven! Oh, mercy! Pixie! Pixie!"

"That's her!" Relief stabbed in his chest. "It's her!"

He shouldered his way past the tangle of figures and equipment in the yard. The front door had been rammed open and two powerful hoses were playing over the smoke and flames that filled the stairwell like a solid column. The front yard seemed overflowing with movement, voices and bulky uniforms. Sirens still wailed. A crowd had gathered in the street, creating more chaos as people blocked the cars of the spectators leaving the fireworks. The air smelled of explosives and burning paint, and the light was unearthly.

But all Patrick saw, and all he heard in this chaos, was Cat, still some distance away. Cat. Precious Cat.

She carried Sam in her arms, and she was trying to run along the uneven sidewalk. Her body was held crookedly, as if she had a stitch in her side. Her breath was heaving. The little boy's legs swung and bumped against hers. The toes of his chunky running shoes had to be bruising her skin. In her panic, she was as awkward as Patrick had been.

When she drew abreast of the next house, she let the child slide to the ground, gasping, "Walk, honey, walk for me now."

Then she began to sprint.

Patrick went to meet her, yelling as he drew near. "It's okay," he said. "Pixie's out. She's safe. And the dog. I think a neighbor's taken him now. But your sisters...your sisters!"

He reached her, took her in his arms without even thinking about it, "Your sisters, Cat."

He shuddered with relief as they touched, then bent and buried his face in the curve of her neck and pulled her hard up against him. For a moment, he actually swung her off the ground, and the adrenaline was surging through him so strongly that he didn't even feel her weight.

"No. It's all right," she said. She was shaking. Didn't fight him off, just stood in his arms, once he'd put her down again. She was trembling like someone in the throes of a convulsion. "They're not here. They had to go to New York. Thank the Lord they're not here!"

"Oh, Cat, yes," he whispered, pushing her hair back from her face, running his hands across her shoulders and down her arms. His face was just an inch from hers. It was as if he needed to make sure she was real by touching her and holding her close. "And thank the Lord you and Sam weren't in the house. I couldn't get an answer from Pixie about it. She was too distraught. And I just kept thinking, were you and the others inside the house? Especially you, Cat, the thought of you, in that smoke, choking and being burned..."

He was kissing her before he knew he was going to do it, tasting the warm life in her lips, using his mouth to still their trembling. Or maybe it was Cat's touch that was bringing him under control, not the other way around.

He didn't stop to question it. He just knew they both needed it, as if the kiss was an affirmation of life itself, after the passing, so close, of death's shadow.

The feel of her, the taste of her, was a miracle. He'd rolled over metal guttering, been embraced by scratchy wisteria, but Cat felt soft, pliant and alive. He had the harsh bitterness of smoke still in his mouth, but she tasted sweet, like apples.

For the first time in his adult life...for the first time since he stopped giving a young child's exuberant lip smacks to his parents and the occasional cousin nearly thirty years ago...this kiss had no planning, no goal, no agenda attached. It felt good...no, it felt *essential*...so he kept doing it.

She moaned with need and release and fear. Opening eyes that had instinctively closed when their lips first touched, he saw that she was frowning, her face tight with stress. Her creamy eyelids were creased and every muscle in her face was locked. He kissed her forehead, kissed her temples, kissed the strain away, then returned to crush his mouth against hers again.

As her trembling eased and her breathing steadied, he unwrapped his arms from around her back and lifted his fingers to her face to stroke her jaw.

"Oh, Cat..." He dragged his mouth from hers just long enough to say her name, then held her hungrily once more, tasted her, filled his hands with her warm, real body, still overwhelmed by the enormity of the tragedy that might have been.

If he'd lost her before he'd even begun to know her, it would have haunted him forever.

"Don't let me go, Patrick," Cat told him shakily. "Just don't."

He was holding her so tightly now that she almost had to push against his chest to breathe, but still it wasn't enough. She needed this. Needed him. The maleness of him, the way he smelled of smoke, almost as if he'd been scorched. Sweat, too, as if he'd been doing hard physical work. She needed the fact that he was so strong and warm and *breathing*. It seemed so right that he was here, a crystallizing of all the times she'd been thinking about him over the past two weeks, without admitting it even to herself.

Suddenly, she realized that she'd dreamed about him. Maybe more than once. It was the kind of dream that evanesced within seconds of waking, to leave a flavor that could scarcely be called a memory. In a way, such dreams were more powerful than the ones which left their details clearly etched.

And in the dream it had been just like this. Darkness, a sense of chaos, and clinging to each other, melting into each other, as if nothing else in the world existed but their two selves. Now. Here.

And he was here because… She tried to grab at something more rational than the fragment of a dream, tried to orient her world once more. He was here because—

Well, obviously he'd been watching the fireworks, or something. Had he parked in her street?

Didn't matter, the logistics of it, she decided, and abandoned the issue. It wasn't important. He was just here.

Then, at the edge of her consciousness, she felt a much smaller pair of arms wrap around her legs and a face come burrowing against her thigh, dampening the fabric of her trouser leg with sweat from his hot face.

"Oh, my lord—Sam!" she gasped.

She turned at once from Patrick's arms and

crouched down beside her nephew, lacing her fingers together around his slim waist, clad in blue jeans. It could only be a minute or so since she'd let him slide to his feet, after she'd carried him at a panicky run for several blocks until her arms had felt as if they were being slowly dragged from their sockets. Those precious seconds in Patrick's arms, moments suspended out of the flow of time, made it seem like far longer.

"The house is burning down," Sam said in a tiny voice. "And Mommy's not here to see."

Cat had to laugh. "To see?"

"She likes fires."

"Bonfires, honey. Barbecue fires. Campfires. Not fires like this." She couldn't suppress a shudder. "Definitely not fires like this!"

Sam began to cry, sensitive to her mood. "Will they fix it, Aunt Cattie?"

"I hope so, sweetie. It's a brick house. It's not going to burn to the ground, but it may be a while before we can live in it again."

"This is your house, sir?"

A senior member of the fire crew, his limbs stiff in his huge, heat-shielding blue-and-yellow uniform jacket had come up to Patrick, evidently recognizing him as someone who had been on the scene.

"No," he answered quickly. "I'm just a friend. Catrina?"

"I live here," she said, straightening and stepping forward. She took a steadying breath. "The house belongs to my cousin."

"Well, we have things under control now," the officer reported soberly. "There's some pretty extensive damage, but it's localized to the staircase area and the front hallway, which is where the blaze seems to have begun. There's extensive smoke damage in the upper level, too''

"I—I don't care about all that right now," Cat said. "I'm sorry. I can't take it in. Where's Pixie?" She turned to Patrick. "You said she was safe."

"The elderly woman?" the fire officer said. "She's being treated for smoke inhalation at this time, and they're preparing to take her to the hospital."

"Can I go along, too? She's frail and she gets upset about things. Can Sam and I—?"

"Not in the ambulance. You can follow along. We'd like to ask you a couple of questions first, if we could."

Cat nodded blindly. Questions. Sure. She couldn't think, could only follow instructions obediently, didn't even realize that she was clinging to Patrick's hard, warm forearm until Sam reached for her again and she had to let go of Patrick to take the child in her arms.

Everything was still chaotic. It all flowed over her, registering in her mind and her senses but not generating a true response. The crowds were ebbing away, but the congestion in the street was still extreme. The emergency vehicles had to run up on the sidewalk in places in order to get through, making ruts in the grass and soft earth and narrowly skirting the bases of the big old trees that shaded the street.

Filthy black water was still gushing from the house, streaming down the slope of the porch and dripping off the edge, muddying the flower beds where green and white hostas and red impatiens grew in the shade. Firemen stomped around in their big boots, shouting questions at each other, checking their equipment.

Cat had Sam on her lap as she sat in the cab of the fire truck while the fire officer stood just outside, leaning one arm in the open doorway. Sam was getting tired and his eyes had glazed a little. Patrick stood near the back of the fire truck in what was apparently the quietest spot he could find, talking into his cell phone with a palm pressed over his free ear to shut out the background noise.

His body looked angular, surging with energy. He was restless and constantly moving. A pace in one direction, three paces back the opposite way. He wheeled around, planted his feet like tree trunks for several seconds, shook his head and paced again.

Cat distractedly told the fire officer, "No, there are no smokers in the house," and then, for the first time, she noted what Patrick was wearing.

Shorts that had once been khaki and a T-shirt that used to be white. Both garments were filthy, streaked brown and black in irregular lines and blotches. There was a three-inch triangular tear at the front of the T-shirt, showing a glimpse of tight, tanned stomach.

As she watched, he absently lifted the hem of the T-shirt and used a big stretch of it to mop the dirt and sweat from his face. Then he yelled something into the phone that she couldn't catch and let the filthy shirt fall again.

My lord, why did he look like that? There was a twig in his hair, a long red scratch down his cheek from temple to jaw, and both his knees were brown and scraped like the knees of a child who'd been playing in the dirt.

"How did Pixie get out of the house? Did she jump?" Cat asked the fire officer suddenly.

He stopped mid-question and shook his head, and Cat already knew what she was going to hear.

"Your friend on the cell phone there pulled her out, I believe," he said. "She was a lucky woman. I'm going to need to talk to him about all of this a little later."

So am I! Cat thought suddenly, her mind clicking back into focus and a rebellious and determined spirit building up inside her. It was the same rebellion that had built two days after the Mirabeau on Ice Ball, when he'd showed up at the ice rink to claim her so casually.

"Damn it," she muttered aloud, through clenched teeth, "So am I!"

"She was very lucky, and she's in good shape considering her age and what she went through," said the nurse in the Intensive Care Unit at the local hospital.

"Then she's going to live?" Cat asked. Pixie looked so frail and gray against the white hospital linen. Sedated, she breathed heavily into her oxygen mask and muttered in her unnatural sleep. She wore a faded hospital gown with a nondescript pattern and her hand was limp in Cat's. "She's—she's really going to be okay?"

She was so scared even to ask the question that the words tasted metallic in her mouth, like blood. She made herself say it all the same. With one year to go in her training to be a nurse, she felt her own medical knowledge like a burden tonight. She knew too much, and her knowledge conjured up a dark cavern of possibilities.

"Yes, to both of those," the nurse said. "But she'll be in here for a few days, because we need to get the effect of all that smoke out of her system."

"I can't stay," Cat realized aloud. She explained, "I want to, to be here when she wakes, but my stepsisters are away, and I have Sam to take care of..."

He had fallen asleep in Patrick's car. Yes, Patrick's car. Cat had only accepted his offer of a ride to the hospital out of sheer desperation. She'd wanted to follow Pixie as quickly as possible. Patrick had carried him up here to the ICU as if he weighed no more than a kitten. Then Sam had stirred and wanted Aunt Cattie so now she had him in her arms once more, his head heavy and hard on her shoulder and his sleep light and fitful, as she sat beside Pixie.

He whimpered whenever he half woke, and she was desperate to get him into a bed, to get on the phone to Jill and Suzanne in New York—and lord knew, they didn't need the news of the fire on top of the earth-shattering reason for their trip to that city!

Suddenly, an image of the gaping, sodden black hole at the front of Pixie's house flashed into her mind and she added another urgent task to her list for tonight. All their possessions, the entire worldly goods of five people, were still in the house, and it was open to anyone who passed by. At least, thank heaven, they'd persuaded innocent, dithery Pixie to insure the place last year, but...

What did you do? You got a construction company to come and board up the opening, or something?

"I have to check into a motel," she told the nurse distractedly. "When I get there, can I call this unit and give you my number so you can update me on how she's doing? If there's any important change in her condition? I'll try to get back here as soon as possible in the morning."

"Sure," the nurse nodded with a reassuring smile. She looked caring, cheerful and intensely capable.

"Here's my home phone number." Patrick was scribbling something on a small rectangle of card. He handed it to the nurse. "Forget the motel. This is where Catrina and Sam will be staying."

Cat didn't argue the point. Not to start with. She went as far as the lobby in Patrick's company, Sam in her arms, her ears ringing with exhaustion and her temples knotted with stress.

Then in the lobby she still didn't argue. She just told him, "I'm not staying with you, Patrick."

"It's a four-bedroom apartment," he explained calmly. "There's a room for you, and one for Sam. Your own bathroom, too."

She ignored him. "I'm taking a cab to the Motel 18 down on Broad and Lincoln."

"Lincoln? I've driven down that street a few times. Motels there rent by the hour."

"Or the month," she retorted.

"Which kind of client are you?" he shot back at her.

"The kind with nowhere else to go."

She glared at him, eyes blazing, felt more vulnerable than she wanted to admit with Sam so heavy in her arms. Patrick had lost the restless energy of the adrenaline now, but if anything it made him seem stronger, more confident, and more at ease.

"I've already said—" he began again.

"And *I've* already said, not tonight but twelve days ago, there's no place for you in my life, Patrick Callahan. I—" She thought of what he'd done tonight, that he'd saved Pixie's life, and felt a stab of discomfort, but she ignored it and went on more firmly, "I don't trust what's going on here. Thanks for what you did. I'll think of a better way to thank you as soon as I can think straight."

"You don't need to."

Once more she ignored him. "But for now, please get on home and get yourself cleaned up. Sam and I are going to sit here and wait for our cab."

Patrick looked at her. He didn't know whether to be angry at her stubbornness, wounded at her mistrust or amazed at her courage. She was so slim and fair. She had those Swiss milkmaid braids in her hair again, and she was wearing another one of those tank-top-and-skimpy-pants-type outfits that made her look like she was about sixteen.

She and Sam would be eaten alive at the Motel 18 on Broad and Lincoln. If not by the mosquitoes that bred thickly in the brackish water inside the tires at the unofficial trash dump just yards away, then by the sleazy clients.

He knew the type of place it was. The ones who paid by the hour were there for the kind of sex he didn't even want to think about, and the ones who paid by the month were, ninety percent of them, users and dealers, ex-cons, short-term "families" who didn't deserve the name.

But, look at her, she was so stubborn and proud. *Like me.*

Stubborn about different things. Proud in a way he'd never needed to be.

Still, it was a kinship. He recognized it even if she didn't, and, damn it, he wasn't going to give up on that connection…or any of the other connections he sensed between them…just yet.

"Want me to call the cab for you?"

"I can do that."

"You going to put Sam down while you make the call?"

Cat looked around and saw what Patrick had already noted. No seats in the lobby, just a couple of aluminum benches out front, out of sight of the phones. She assented reluctantly to his offer, and he chalked it up as a small victory.

"Might be a bit of a wait at this time of night," he said. The hands on the clock behind the main reception desk had each just crawled their way past the one.

"I can handle it," she said.

"I could drop you at the motel."

"I'd rather wait. You've already done enough." It sounded almost like an accusation, but he let it slide.

"I'll call the cab company from my cell phone," he said instead. "And I'll be in to visit your cousin sometime in the morning. Maybe I'll see you then."

"You don't need to—"

This time, he *didn't* let it slide.

"Listen, Cat." His voice fell heavily into the air between them. "I rolled your cousin out of a burning house tonight."

"I—I know."

"It wasn't a particularly elegant rescue, but I saved her life. You can put whatever limits you like on any dealings you and I have with each other, but when one person saves another person's life, there's a link, a bond, and I'm not prepared to ignore that. I'm going to visit with Pixie tomorrow whether you want me to or not. And for you to deny me that because of the line *you've* decided to draw in the sand regarding the chemistry between us would just be wrong. You can see that, can't you?"

Her eyes narrowed. There was a small silence, and then she nodded, the movement almost puppet-like. Hell, she was totally exhausted!

"I'm sorry, Patrick," she said. "On that point you're right. I was out of line, and I apologize. Of course you should see Pixie in the morning. Maybe I'll see you there."

They said a brief goodbye to each other, then she crossed to the automatic doors, hefting Sam higher on her hip and shoulder with a degree of effort, Patrick saw. He wondered what was keeping her going—sheer will?—and considered actually man-handling Sam out of her arms and kidnapping the child in order to get her to see sense and come home with him, but he dismissed the idea.

He admired a little stubbornness in a woman, he discovered. Cat and Sam needed a safety net tonight, and he had an inkling that she would recognize the fact pretty soon, stubbornness notwithstanding. When she did, he'd make sure to be there. Until then, he could only accept that she would follow her own course.

Chapter Six

"Okay, here's the key. Number 225, top floor. We can do you a weekly rate, but you hafta tell the desk by ten in the morning, or tonight don't count for that and it's full price. Tell the desk if the toilet stops up again, but save your breath till the morning, 'cause there's no one to fix it tonight."

"Uh-huh." Cat nodded, her stomach sinking.

"Have a pleasant stay." The words were so flat and insincere that the slovenly woman standing behind the desk barely bothered to open her mouth to say them.

Cat shouldered open the creaking door of the motel office and let herself out to face the bevy of waiting mosquitoes, the way a scandal-prone actress would have faced the paparazzi. She ignored the ones that settled on her own face, arms and neck, but batted at the ones attacking Sam until she accidentally connected with his cheek. It was almost a slap and he woke abruptly, gasped in shock and began to cry.

"Oh, honey, I'm sorry! I'm so sorry! It was the mosquitoes, not you."

"Where are we?"

"Our motel, sweetie."

She toiled up the stained and pitted concrete stairs at the end of the building, then heard shouting and screams break out farther along. Distracted by the string of shrieked curse words, she almost stumbled over an inert body sprawled on the landing of the stairs. There was a groan and more swearing, which trailed off into heavy breathing. The stench of stale alcohol breached her nostrils, and she moved on hastily.

She passed an open doorway, glanced in automatically and saw several people flung out on beds and on the floor, staring with glazed expressions at a flickering TV screen. Her spirits died and she felt sick. At the hospital, the cab hadn't come for forty-five minutes. It was almost ten after two now. This place made the trailer park that she and her sisters used to live in seem like a five-star gated community.

The shouting continued along the cement walkway, and when she counted off the shabby numbers on the doors she realized that the domestic dispute was coming from the room right next to number 225.

Oh, mercy, Sam, please go back to sleep! she begged her little nephew silently, but how could he? He was fully awake now, disoriented, round-eyed and scared.

Stomach heaving, Cat turned the key in the cheap

lock, opened the door and was greeted by a waft of mildew and ancient cigarette smoke. She took a last breath of the comparatively fresh air of the balcony, taking in a mosquito at the same time, and tortured herself with a litany of ifs.

If I hadn't left my purse hanging on the stair rail to get burned. It had some extra cash in it, enough for a better place than this. If Suzanne and Jill hadn't had to go to New York. I told them to stay somewhere decent, even though that put each of our bank accounts at next to zero. If I had a credit card....

But, after years of her stepmother Rose's perpetually maxed-out cards, she and her stepsisters had made a decision to keep to a cash budget. It had kept them solvent for six years, but it didn't help now. This appalling place had been her only choice.

Her only choice, that is, apart from Patrick Callahan. What would Jill say about the fact that Cat had rejected his help, when Sam's well-being was at stake?

Another screaming set of curses erupted from the room next door, and Sam renewed his tears, sobs of fear this time, not just of fatigue.

Cat heard steady footsteps behind her, and turned in time to see a pair of brilliant blue eyes and hear a familiar voice telling her in a tone of intense frustration, "For Sam's sake, Cat, if for no other reason, will you come to my place now?"

"Yes," she stammered. "Lord, yes, I'll come now. I didn't think it would be this bad. I hoped he'd just sleep through it. Sam, honey, we're not going to stay here after all. You don't have to be scared anymore."

She kissed his soft dark hair, dizzy with relief.

"Want to give your Aunt Cattie's arms a rest and come to me?" Patrick said to Sam, his voice calm and cheerful and easy. "She made a mistake and came to the wrong place, but it's okay now. Just leave the key in the room, Cat. You paid in advance, right?"

She nodded.

Patrick took Sam with the ease of practice. Cat recognized it and was surprised. Somehow, he didn't look like a man who knew about kids. And Sam at once recognized a friend.

He snuggled into Patrick's capable, muscled arms as if he were snuggling into a soft mattress and said with innocent happiness, "You smell nice. Like pine trees and lemonade."

Patrick laughed, and this was the dominant sound in Cat's ears as they walked away from the ugly room. Not the sour cursing of strangers, but Patrick Callahan's warm, rich laugh.

"It's about twenty minutes to my apartment at this time of night," he said.

He had parked his car directly beside the stairs, and there were a couple of figures slouched in the doorway of a room in the other wing of the motel, across the asphalt lot, already eyeing the vehicle with interest. Theft, maybe? Or vandalism? Either way, Patrick ignored them totally, not even troubling to flex his well-honed muscles for their benefit.

His muscles, covered by...

Cat did a double take as she slid into the expensive vehicle. "You've changed," she accused him.

He was wearing dark pants and a navy T-shirt now, both garments fresh and uncreased. They clung to the strong lines and planes of his figure, emphasizing his powerful frame. His face was freshly washed and shaven, and he had a Band-Aid on the deepest section of the scratch she'd noticed earlier.

"You're *clean!*" she went on. "Then you didn't just follow me here?"

"What, spying on you at every turn?" He eased Sam out of his arms, nestled him into the corner of the rear seat, covered him with a soft blanket, and snapped his seat belt. "No, I didn't follow you here. I went home, had a shower. Thought you might need to settle in for a bit before you saw sense."

He started the engine and wheeled the car around. "Cab must have taken longer than I thought."

"Forty-five minutes. On the other hand, I saw sense a lot quicker."

"You did," he agreed. "Are you going to let me say I told you so?"

"No."

"Didn't think so."

"You'd like to wring every possible drop of remorse and regret from me tonight, is that it?" she said, trying to keep it light.

"No, Cat," he answered seriously. "I'm just trying to establish a workable baseline for our dealings with each other, that's all. I know you didn't want to do this. Didn't want to need me. I understand that. I didn't engineer the situation, and I'm not going to try and milk your gratitude. The fire happened. You needed me and so did Sam. Doesn't mean we can't be equals. Okay?"

"Okay," she said quietly.

Inwardly, she was stunned at the way he'd laid his cards—and hers—right out on the table, and taken the fight out of her at the same time. Was he right? Saying it like that, straight down the line with no frills or false promises, it seemed like he had to be.

Turning, she saw that Sam had already fallen asleep in the back seat. The purr of the powerful car lulled her as they drove, and by the time they reached Patrick's apartment building, which she recognized as the best high-rise address in the greater Philadelphia area, she was on the point of dozing herself.

It took only a few minutes to get Sam settled on a sofa bed in the room that Patrick obviously used as his private gym. There were weights, a treadmill, a sit-up bench. Sam practically sleepwalked through a visit to the bathroom, a half a glass of milk and a peel down to T-shirt and underwear.

Then he snuggled into sheets that smelled, like Patrick himself, of pine trees and lemonade. He drifted off at once with a soft smile on his face.

Cat had to blink back tears as she tiptoed out of the room. Sam was safe and happy and peaceful at last. Poor Jill didn't know anything about all this yet. She'd hated having to leave him for the three nights she and Suzanne planned to be in New York.

Jill hugged her son extra close to her heart these days. Almost four months ago, she'd left him with Cat and Suzanne and Pixie for six weeks to skate in a Las Vegas ice show, but the whole experience had been a huge watershed for her. She'd hated the show, realized that her whole dream of show-skating as a career was a chimera.

She couldn't mesh that lifestyle with doing her best for Sam, and Sam was what really counted in her life, Jill had found. There had been deep, genuine changes in her when she got back from Vegas, not all of which, Cat sensed, Jill had yet put into words.

Now, she was training in office work, and she'd begun to date the widowed father of two of her former skating students. Alan Jennings was a man in his forties who had security for his kids at the very top of his priorities, and Jill was now convinced that this was the only thing that counted. She seemed focused, if not exactly happy, and she'd handled the tragedy in New York with new maturity.

"I want to take Sam," she'd said. "But I know I can't. I mean, it's my half-sister's funeral. Suzanne and I hadn't even told Sam about Jodie's existence yet, since even for us it was still so new and hard to take in. That Mom—" Cat's stepmother, Rose "—had given away a baby at seventeen and never said a word about it for thirty-seven years, till Jodie herself got in touch with us in April. And now the aneurysm, and she's dead. I can't tell him about it yet."

So Sam was here with Aunt Cattie while Suzanne and Jill attended their half-sister's funeral and visited Jodie's premature newborn in the hospital.

Hospitals… Cousin Pixie…the fire…Patrick's rescue…

Overwhelmed, and holding herself together by a thread, Cat closed the door behind her and went to find Patrick.

"Shower first, then scrambled eggs and bacon on toast," he told her, cracking eggs into a bowl in his state-of-the-art kitchen.

Recessed ceiling lights reflected off stainless steel and brought out the sparkles in a slab of gray granite. A vast stainless-steel fridge and freezer unit hummed. It reminded Cat of the O.R. at the large hospital where she'd interned last summer. Not warm. Too practical. It wasn't until the bacon began to sizzle and heat rose from the blue gas flames on the stove—stainless steel, again—that the room began to feel like a kitchen.

"I don't usually eat eggs and bacon at three in the morning," she protested.

"Don't usually have half your house burned down while you're out watching fireworks, either."

"The fireworks! Lord, I never thought! Was it a stray rocket that set off the fire, then? But—"

"No, it wasn't," he said shortly, and she had started to wonder why he sounded so tense about it when another thought flew by, distracting her.

"I haven't called anyone yet!" she said. "Carpenters or someone, to nail up the front. It was gaping, and all our stuff is—"

"Relax," he said. "It's taken care of."

"Wh-?" She shook her head.

"Earlier tonight I called a friend who runs a construction company. Before we even followed Pixie to the hospital. By now it's all boarded up and they've gone home. Take your shower or these eggs'll be ready before you are."

She nodded blankly. "Where—?"

"Cross the living room, into the hall, second door on the left."

"Uh, thanks."

"Part of the service."

Thick fluffy grey towels, and a dazzling array of pale soaps, shampoos, bath oils and lotions were evidently part of the service, also. Cat kept it simple,

An Important Message
from the Editors

Dear Reader,

Because you've chosen to read one of our fine romance novels, we'd like to say "thank you!" And, as a special way to thank you, we've selected two more of the books you love so well, plus an exciting Mystery Gift, to send you absolutely FREE!

Please enjoy them with our compliments...

Pam Powers

P.S. And because we value our customers, we've attached something extra inside...

Peel off seal and place inside...

EDITOR'S
FREE GIFT
SEAL
THANK YOU

How to validate your Editor's
FREE GIFT
"Thank You"

1. Peel off gift seal from front cover. Place it in space provided at right. This automatically entitles you to receive 2 FREE BOOKS and a fabulous mystery gift.

2. Send back this card and you'll get 2 brand-new Silhouette Romance® novels. These books have a cover price of $3.99 each in the U.S. and $4.50 each in Canada, but they are yours to keep absolutely free.

3. There's no catch. You're under no obligation to buy anything. We charge nothing—ZERO—for your first shipment. And you don't have to make any minimum number of purchases—not even one!

4. The fact is, thousands of readers enjoy receiving their books by mail from the Silhouette Reader Service™. They enjoy the convenience of home delivery...they like getting the best new novels at discount prices BEFORE they're available in stores...and they love their *Heart to Heart* subscriber newsletter featuring author news, horoscopes, recipes, book reviews and much more!

5. We hope that after receiving your free books you'll want to remain a subscriber. But the choice is yours—to continue or cancel, any time at all! So why not take us up on our invitation, with no risk of any kind. You'll be glad you did!

6. Don't forget to detach your FREE BOOKMARK. And remember...just for validating your Editor's Free Gift Offer, we'll send you THREE gifts, *ABSOLUTELY FREE!*

GET A FREE MYSTERY GIFT

YOURS FREE!

SURPRISE MYSTERY GIFT COULD BE YOURS _FREE_ AS A SPECIAL "THANK YOU" FROM THE EDITORS OF SILHOUETTE

Visit us online at
www.eHarlequin.com

PLACE
FREE GIFT
SEAL
HERE

YES! I have placed my Editor's "Thank You" seal in the space provided above. Please send me 2 free books and a fabulous mystery gift. I understand I am under no obligation to purchase any books, as explained on the back and on the opposite page.

315 SDL DC3G

215 SDL DC3C
(S-R-OS-09/01)

NAME   (PLEASE PRINT CLEARLY)

ADDRESS

APT.#   CITY

STATE/PROV.   ZIP/POSTAL CODE

Thank You!

DETACH AND MAIL CARD TODAY!

The Silhouette Reader Service™ — Here's how it works:

Accepting your 2 free books and gift places you under no obligation to buy anything. You may keep the books and gift and return the shipping statement marked "cancel." If you do not cancel, about a month later we'll send you 6 additional novels and bill you just $3.15 each in the U.S., or $3.50 each in Canada, plus 25¢ shipping & handling per book and applicable taxes if any.* That's the complete price and — compared to cover prices of $3.99 each in the U.S. and $4.50 each in Canada — it's quite a bargain! You may cancel at any time, but if you choose to continue, every month we'll send you 6 more books, which you may either purchase at the discount price or return to us and cancel your subscription.

*Terms and prices subject to change without notice. Sales tax applicable in N.Y. Canadian residents will be charged applicable provincial taxes and GST.

soaped herself with an almond-scented seashell
shape, rinsed her hair through with plain water and
was out in five minutes.

The eggs were ready, set on matte black plates on
the countertop, with triangles of toast and bacon so
crisp it could shatter.

Cat had begun to sense a theme in Patrick's apartment, as far as colors went. Basically, there weren't
any. She shivered for a moment in the air-
conditioning, then turned and scanned the living
room and saw a gorgeous original oil painting, a
warm, textured abstract pattern in tones of terracotta,
crimson, pink, cinnamon and blue. She felt better.
There was warmth in this designer-decorated, mil-
lion-dollar apartment after all. The place just needed
a few more touches of home, a little more that said,
"I'm lived in."

*As if it's my concern that his apartment feels a
little cold.*

"Sit down," Patrick invited her. "I'll bring it
in."

He came out of the kitchen to set a filled plate in
front of her, then sat down with his own at the glass-
topped dining table in the open-plan living room. At
this point, Cat discovered that he was right. She was
starving. She polished off eggs, bacon and toast as
fast as a puppy with a greedy brother, then looked
up to see Patrick grinning at her.

She flushed, opened her mouth and searched for
an excuse, but he got in first.

"I appreciate a gal who knows how to eat."

"And I guess I'd have to say I appreciate a guy
who knows a gal's hungry before she knows it herself."

He laughed and she grinned back at him, despite her best intentions. She'd never known before how good it could feel to get a man to laugh, especially when he had a laugh like Patrick's, so rich and deep and honest.

Then her gaze locked with his and the electricity of their intuitive connection arced between them. It was so strong that she could practically see the sizzle, and it made her heart pound and her breathing get shallow. Heat began to pool low inside her.

To break the moment, she said, "I'll clean up."

"Don't bother. There's not much to do."

But she grabbed both their plates anyway and skimmed into the kitchen. She couldn't immediately find the dishwasher, as it was camouflaged by all those acres of stainless steel. Instead, she put the plates down with fluttering hands on a piece of granite countertop, turned and cannoned straight into him.

Had he intended to kiss her all along? She wasn't sure about that, but he was certainly happy to seize the opportunity when it came.

It wasn't a huge kiss. He simply brushed his mouth across hers—she tasted warmth and salt— then said softly, stroking her shoulders, "Leave it! Go to bed! Your room is next to Sam's. Goodnight, Cat."

He brushed her mouth again, and this time his lips parted so that she felt a tiny dab of moisture paint her mouth. Enveloped in his clean, fresh scent, she felt a stab of desire, physical and very female, thrusting through her. Her need and her response were so close to the surface that one more touch from him would have stripped back her resistance to the bone.

And he knew it! Oh, he had to!

He was a sophisticated, experienced man, far more sophisticated than she was. More important, he was wealthy, successful, accustomed to control, not the kind of man who ever had to take no for an answer in his daily life. She'd already said no to him more than once, yet here she was in spite of that, exactly as he'd wanted.

As if it was all planned.

And, oh my lord, it was after three in the morning and she was tired, tired. She'd almost lost her home, and Pixie had almost lost her life. Two hours away in New York City, her stepsisters, so close to her that most of the time she never considered the "step" part at all, were going through a shattering event of their own. She hadn't even told Patrick about it yet.

With all this, maybe it wasn't surprising that Cat suddenly *lost* it. Just completely lost it. She backed away from him, wiped the back of her hand hard across her mouth to wipe away his kiss and glared at him with blazing eyes.

"So tell me what you were doing, Patrick, coming down my street at ten o'clock on firecracker night, at exactly the right moment to save my cousin from that blazing house! Are you going to try telling me it was on your route to work? Did you have me watched, these past two weeks? Did you watch me yourself? Are you stalking me, Patrick? Maybe you're really crazy and you lit that fire yourself!"

"It's a possibility the fire department's arson squad is looking into," he answered calmly.

She ignored him. "I said no to you at the Mirabeau Ball, Patrick, and I said it again two days later when you came back to the rink. I didn't trust what you wanted from me back then, and I still don't. So why are you still in my life?"

He took a big, jagged breath, and for a moment she thought he was going to yell right back at her. Then he said instead, not quite angry, not quite offhand, "Which question do you want me to answer first?"

"Did you set that fire?" she shot back at him, after a fraction of a second's pause for thought.

"No. But I think I saw the man who did. And the last three digits of his license plate stuck in my mind. I've already told that to the arson squad."

"Arson!" Cat put her fingers to her temples, where every muscle had suddenly tightened. "It *was* deliberately lit? Who would want—?"

She sank back against the cold, hard edge of the countertop, her legs drained of their strength and her mind buzzing harshly.

Patrick watched her intently without moving, but she sensed he was poised to step in and support her if she began to crumple. For several seconds, it was a distinct possibility, but she spread her hands to each side of her, gripped the countertop and regained control.

"Think back to your Cinderella conspiracy at the ball, Lady Catrina," he said softly. "It's doubtful that Councillor Wainwright has announced the direction of his vote just yet, since he knows it's the vote that will decide the whole issue. Someone still trusts that the rezoning is going to go through. But you told me Pixie didn't want to sell. Someone's trying to make sure she changes her mind. He picked a good night for it, didn't he? Everyone out watching the fireworks, street deserted, and the air full of noise and smoke. Of course it wasn't an accident. It was very well planned."

"Barry Grindlay…"

"Some underling of his, probably, paid for the job. I'll help the police to prove it if I can. They think they'll be able to make use of that partial plate. Next question?"

"*Next—?*"

"You have to focus, here, Cat," he insisted. "You've got some major concerns. If you think we're going to get distracted and not deal with them, you're wrong."

She stared at him. He was serious! The greatest surprise came when she realized that she respected him for it. He was trying to play the whole thing as straight as he could. It didn't seem to be a game.

Didn't *seem* to be…

"What were you doing in my street?"

Once more, his answer came back lightning fast. "Trying to work out why I can't get you out of my head. Trying to decide whether I should respect what you told me nearly two weeks ago, or challenge it. Trying to work out the best way to ask you out so you'd actually accept."

"Patrick, you don't want to go out with me."

"Yes, I do. But if you want to stay in, we can do that, too."

"I don't trust this."

"I know. But at least you feel it. That's a start. We can work with it."

He grinned suddenly, disarming her. She grinned

back helplessly. How could anyone not respond to that smile? It was the smile of a winner, confident and satisfied, and he clearly took her response as some kind of victory for him. Maybe he was right to. She was too tired and too confused about everything she felt to think about it anymore tonight.

He must have seen the fatigue wash over her.

"You can go to bed now," he told her.

"Gee, thanks!"

"Sleep on it, okay?"

She didn't answer, just gave a tiny nod and stumbled across the living room and down the hallway to her room.

Pixie was giggling the next day when Cat and Sam caught sight of her through the doorway of her hospital room. Patrick sat in the chair beside her bed, telling her what was apparently an incredibly funny story.

Pixie's laugh was still harsh and her breathing difficult, but she was out of the ICU and her color was far better than Cat had dared to hope for.

"Hi, Aunt Pixie!" Sam said, coming forward.

Hearing his little voice, Patrick turned, and Cat was immediately conscious once again of the pull between them. Every time he looked at her, his blue eyes seemed to say it.

You feel this. Admit it. Tell me I'm right.

She hardened her heart. When you were a winner by nature, like Patrick Callahan, you didn't pick and choose your contests. You wanted to win at every game you played, no matter how trivial to you, or how important to someone else.

Once he had won this one, however, what next?

A new game, no doubt, with a different goal. At that point, the feelings he'd begun to coax out of her would be left in the dust.

She'd seen it happen before, to Jill. And she'd heard too often from Rose the bitterness and dissatisfaction that came when the game's winner was stuck with a prize he or she no longer valued.

Cat had been just two years old when her mother had died. When she was four, her father had married Rose, whose first marriage, also "beneath her level," had produced her daughters Suzanne and Jill.

David Brown was a good man in all the ways that really counted. He was a loving and sensible father and stepfather, and a steady worker and provider, despite his lack of formal education. But beautiful, shallow Rose hadn't valued those things. Even the quietly magnetic good looks that had initially attracted her had soon lost their power to charm, leaving her to moan for nearly thirteen years about her "mistake" and his "worthlessness."

"When I think of the men I could have had," came the familiar lament. "Well-bred, wealthy..."

Cat's father, with much greater cause for disappointment in Rose's shallow personality, had held his tongue, never betrayed his unhappiness, and quietly died after a short illness. Cat had been just seventeen, Jill a few months older and Suzanne, twenty. Rose had waited a token year before deciding that it was no longer her duty to provide Cat with a home...

"Honey, how's my baby Giselle?" Pixie said to Cat, gripping her hand and wheezing as she spoke.

Oh, mercy, I never even thought to check! Cat

thought. I know Mrs. Mark next door took her and kept her safe, but beyond that…. There's just been so much else.

She had woken late, checked on Sam, who was still asleep, and discovered that Patrick had left a note for her, along with a wad of cash for cab fares. This she had ignored.

Not wanting breakfast, she'd phoned her sisters at their hotel in New York. She'd told them the news about the fire, answering their shocked questions as best she could. They'd had news of their own to add to the turmoil.

Jodie's frail newborn would survive the traumatic emergency of her Caesarean birth and would achieve full health, with the right medical treatment, but she would need a stay of weeks or even months in the hospital. The baby had been conceived through artificial insemination, so there was no father on the scene to claim her. Through prenatal testing, Jodie had known the child would be a girl and had already chosen her name—Alice, after Jodie's adoptive parents, Alex and Lisette.

No one yet knew who would raise Alice, Suzanne had said. It was all up in the air, unresolved.

But even over the phone, Cat could hear the determination in her elder stepsister's voice. Maybe Suzanne hadn't even articulated it to herself yet, but Cat knew that she fully intended to adopt that baby herself.

After finishing the conversation with her sisters, Cat had called Pixie's insurance company about putting in a claim, trying to think practically about the future. They needed to get things organized. And they needed to get back into the house as soon as possible. How could they afford to live anywhere else?

She had woken Sam, fed him some cereal and toast in Patrick's kitchen, and they'd caught buses together. Two to get from Patrick's to Pixie's, where they surveyed the boarded-up housefront in silence, then went quickly away. The house looked secure, nothing to worry about there, but it was lonely and dark and it reeked of smoke. Another bus had taken them to the hospital, and they'd arrived here just at noon.

To discover Patrick wangling his charming way into innocent Cousin Pixie's heart.

"Giselle is fine," he was saying to her. "Just fine. On my way in here, I called in on your neighbor. Joan, isn't it? Mrs. Mark?"

"Yes?"

"And she said Giselle is perfectly all right. Mrs. Mark gave her a bath this morning to get the smell of smoke out of her coat. She was a little shaky last night, but Mrs. Mark has set up a basket for her, and she ate this morning as usual."

Pixie closed her eyes and two tears squeezed out from beneath her lids.

"That's wonderful. That you would think to check on her for me. That you would pull me out of the smoke and flames the way you did. I don't know how to thank you," she said, shaking her head. Cat could see that Pixie was beginning to get really upset about this issue, the way she could get seriously upset about small things at times. "I just don't know how," she repeated on a tearful squeak.

Patrick could see it, too. He took her papery little hand and squeezed it. "Let's think, now," he said.

"To thank me..." He looked at her as if to size up her entire personality, and his guess was inspired. "How are you at baking?"

"Why, I'm *great* at baking!"

"Thought you might be. Bake me a cake, then. I haven't tasted a home-baked cake in a while. Something with a ton of chocolate that I can eat when it's still slightly warm from the oven."

Pixie opened her eyes. The tears had gone and they were lit up and she was smiling. "I'll do that," she said. "Why, yes, that's just exactly what I'll do! It'd be the perfect thing."

"How did you do that?" Cat asked Patrick in an accusing tone an hour later as they left Pixie to her two hours of compulsory rest.

Sam tagged along. He was holding Cat's hand hard, and he was extremely ready for his lunch. They would eat in the hospital cafeteria. Patrick's idea. He was paying. Also his idea. Cat planned to write down every cent he spent on her and Sam, and pay it back later. With interest. And anonymously if necessary.

"Do what?" Patrick asked innocently.

"Wrap Cousin Pixie around your little finger like that."

"Did I?"

"She was eating out of your hand."

"While wrapped around my little finger?"

"Exactly! Like a pet monkey, or something. Most people...well, most people think she's a little crazy. She isn't, she's just, you know, sort of daffy, and—well, but they don't understand that, and they don't listen to her concerns. They just dismiss them."

"That sounds a little rude."

"It is! But somehow you understood right away. About the cake. Something she could do that was special and concrete, without costing her a fortune. That was so...so *right*."

Again, it sounded like an accusation. In the middle of her gratitude, she was furious with him, and didn't mind letting him know it. *Needed* to let him know it, actually, as a kind of protection against everything else she could feel if she let herself.

"And when she wanted to know how we'd met, you told it to her step-by-step, because somehow you knew she wouldn't follow the story otherwise. That was—well, thanks, I guess. I'm grateful...and I really, *really* wish you wouldn't keep doing it!"

"Because you'd prefer it if I was a jerk, right?" he queried calmly.

"Right."

"I knew you were stubborn," he said with great complacency. "It's one of the things we have in common."

"It isn't!"

"It is."

"I bet I can be a lot more stubborn than you!"

"And proud. And competitive. Both of us."

"So we argue, every two minutes. Great!"

"Zesty, isn't it?"

She scowled at him and he grinned back, and the grin shot straight to her heart, then arrowed even farther down and made her quiver inside. The score at the moment? She'd lost track, but at a guess, Callahan six, Brown two.

The hospital dining room was quiet today. Cat ordered herself and Sam each a tunafish salad sandwich because they were cheap, then let Patrick buy Sam a dish of ice cream and lime Jell-O because she couldn't punish a four-year-old child for her own stupidity in feeling helplessly attracted to a man whom she knew would affect her well-being about as positively as a comet ramming into the Earth. Serenely unaware of the dark reasoning behind his treat, Sam enjoyed every spoonful.

"Am I allowed to give the two of you a lift back to my place, or are you itching for more bus rides?" Patrick asked cheerfully after they'd eaten.

"Um…"

"I came back home this morning to drive you here, and saw you getting onto the 109 bus. Do we have to have these little tussles every couple of hours? You're going to be staying with me for at least a week—"

"We're not!"

"See? Tussles! If you like, I'll charge you rent. And car hire."

"Car hire?"

"I have a second vehicle you're welcome to borrow."

"Pixie's car will be out of the shop tomorrow. Jill and Suzanne get back Tuesday with the Buick. I mean, if it doesn't die on them on the way," Cat felt compelled to add, in the interests of honesty.

"Too much detail, Cat," Patrick murmured. Still focused on his ice cream, Sam wasn't listening. "Boring. When a man sets a woman up as his mistress, he doesn't want to get that much detail, okay? He just wants the gloss."

"Sets up as—!"

"That's what you're thinking, isn't it? That's what you think my angle is."

"Yes!"

"Well, it's annoying, okay? *Real* annoying!" he said. "Let it rest. Plan on paying me back, if you want, but plan on staying till you can go back to your cousin's place. She and your stepsisters are welcome, too."

"Darn it, Patrick Callahan, are you always this hospitable?"

"To decent people who get their home torched by an arsonist for a developer's financial gain? I think I can safely say, always!"

Chapter Seven

There were toys scattered all over the floor of Patrick's living room when he got home from work on Monday evening at six. Really cool toys.

He took a closer look.

No, actually the toys were quite ordinary on their own. Nothing high-tech. No batteries required. But the way they were set up withstood his scorching scrutiny and confirmed his first impression. Really cool.

Natural-toned blocks, homemade from offcuts of wood added to a brightly painted store-bought set to create a town. There were "logs" in different sizes and thicknesses, cut from twigs and branches and laid out to make bridges and edge roads. There were cars on the roads, and construction vehicles set up in a quarry, ready to load piles of beans—several kinds, ranging from small brown lentils to red kidney beans.

Some pieces of green cloth were draped over several of the throw pillows from his couch to make mountains, and there was a blue silk scarf winding through the center of the town forming a river.

Unrelated to any of this, a delectably savory smell wafted to his nostrils from the kitchen.

"Anybody home?"

Patrick was wondering the same thing, but that was his mother's voice, calling from outside his front door. For some reason she rarely rang the bell like normal people, and he knew that if he'd lived in the kind of place that had a back door, Beth Callahan would invariably have used that. Without knocking first.

He loved her, and she drove him nuts.

"Yo, Mom," he called and went to let her in, wondering how in heaven's name he was going to explain the miniature landscape set out on his living room carpet.

It pretty quickly emerged that no such explanation would be necessary, because right behind Mom, just emerging from the elevator, were the explanations themselves, Cat and Sam.

Cat at once looked stricken. "I meant to get home before you did, Patrick," she said. "I'm sorry, it's a mess in there, and you have company and—"

"It looks great."

"Oh, you saw it?"

"I'm home. I mean, I got home a few minutes ago. I'm just letting Mom in."

Cat nodded silently, while Mom's face dropped instantly into her most transparent, "Okay, so are you going to marry my son, or what?" expression. Having seen her eye—he calculated quickly—say, probably, eleven of his past girlfriends with this expression over the course of the past fifteen years or so, Patrick knew it all too well.

Inwardly, he winced.

He wasn't known as Callahan Systems' resident schmoozer for nothing, however.

"Mom, this is Catrina and her nephew Sam, who had a fire damage their house, so they have no place to stay for a few days."

There. That about covered all the necessary data, and, he hoped, stamped out all dangerous sparks of parental curiosity.

"Catrina," he went on, "This is my mom, Beth Callahan, who's not as scary as she looks. Are you, Mom?" he added pointedly.

"If you say so, dear," Mom answered humbly. Good, she'd recognized his cryptic warning. No more questions!

"Are you coming in?" he asked her, not as graciously as he could have.

His mother had raised eight sons, and was now kicking back and enjoying her new and growing crop of granddaughters. It would take about four seconds, once she saw what Cat and Sam had done to his living room, for her to get down on her knees and start loading up a toy dump truck with great northern beans.

Sam would love her, she would love Sam, and the terrifying din of wedding bells would start sounding in Patrick's ears. He knew the scenario. It had happened before. And somehow the recent ideal marriages of two of his brothers and the impending nuptials of a third didn't take the heat off, just made it worse.

What was it about mothers and their first-born

sons? The whole deal could be summed up in one word. Expectations.

They were expectations he'd spent his entire adult life determined not to fulfil, and if he'd begun to have a change of heart on that front, his mother was *not* going to be the first woman to know about it.

No, indeed. Cat was.

Cat was.

He didn't have time to think about it now. Didn't know if it was a crazy whim or a piece of major intuition. Had he just articulated a fairly momentous goal, here? *To marry Catrina Brown.*

Or had Mom successfully hypnotized him at last? *Arrgghhh!*

"No, I'm not coming in," Mom answered him. *Whew!*

She went on, "I really just came to slip the spare keys to Tom's place under your door. Are you..." she glanced at Cat "...still planning to go up next weekend?"

Sheesh, I'd forgotten all about it! He'd been planning a weekend of masculine solitude at his brother's island vacation home on an Adirondack lake in upstate New York since the spring.

"Uh, yeah," he answered, and took the envelope containing the keys. "Thanks."

"I really have to apologize again about the mess," Cat said a few minutes later, when Mrs. Callahan had gone and they were standing together surveying the intricate little landscape once again. "That's why you didn't want your mother to come in, isn't it? Uh, she seems nice, by the way."

Warm and down to earth, and not the intimidating

society matron Cat had instinctively expected. Not that she'd say this to Patrick.

"You got it." He was grinning at her. "She would have started playing, and we'd never have gotten rid of her."

She didn't believe him, Patrick saw. Thought he was just being polite and that he hated the mess.

She said quickly, "Sam, let's pack it all up, honey." She took the little boy's hand and was soon down on the carpet with him, gathering up trucks. "Can you grab the truck tub, Sammy?"

"Ow-w-w..." Sam whined. Then he sighed and went reluctantly on hands and knees to one of the three plastic storage tubs stacked against the wall. The disappointment on his face was painfully apparent.

"Why don't you leave it out to play with again tomorrow?" Patrick heard himself say.

He was rewarded with Sam's instant smile of relief.

Cat protested, but he overrode her. "Looks like you went to such a lot of trouble over it, Sam. It's great. I'd like to see what you do with the bulldozers and the beans."

"Okay," the little brown-haired boy said happily, and launched into an elaborate demonstration of pushing and lifting and dumping. It soon turned into focused play, leaving Patrick free to talk with Cat.

"I hope you don't mind that we brought some of his toys over," she said.

"My living room floor never looked so good," he answered.

She searched his face. "You really do mean that, don't you?"

"You'd know if I didn't." He changed the subject. "Tell me, though, what's cooking?"

"Chili. Sam's favorite. But I forgot to get beans and some other stuff, so we had to go back to the store."

"Seems to me I see a lot of beans right here on the carpet."

"The kind that come in cans, we needed, not the kind that take all day to soak. Plus you don't want to think about how long Sam's been using these particular beans as gravel and rocks and sand. I made enough chili for all of us. If I can just add the beans now, we can eat in a half hour."

"You don't have to cook. I'd have ordered take-out."

"Thanks, but I'd like to try and keep to a regular routine. Sam's used to home cooking."

They went into the kitchen together, and Patrick unpacked the shopping bags while Cat opened the big can of beans. She had bought orange juice, milk, cereal, grape jelly and bananas as well.

"Still missing his mom?"

"A little. And he's still shaken up about the house." Her face brightened. "We took a good look at it today, though. Went over it with the head of the construction crew. Thanks so much for organizing that, Patrick!"

"Wasn't hard," he answered her. "Bill Taylor is an old friend, and I know he's good. He restores and renovates a lot of old places, and he pays attention to detail. How much work does he think it's going to be?"

She glopped the can of beans into the half-cooked chili, then switched on the gas beneath the pot. It roared for a second or two, then she turned it down to low.

"That's what I was going to tell you," she said. "We were lucky. Pixie's a bit manic about closing doors when she goes to bed, so the staircase and front hall were pretty much isolated from the other rooms downstairs. The kitchen and the living areas and the downstairs bathroom are all fine. There's a lingering odor, but if I clean and vacuum, and launder the curtains and cushion covers, it should go."

"That's not so bad, then."

"The staircase itself is burned out and needs replacing," she went on. "So does the ceiling in the hallway, and all the plaster work. There's smoke damage all through the bedrooms, so it'll be a while before we can use those. But we can camp downstairs as soon as they get the gas back on, and that should happen by the end of the week. Monday or Tuesday at the latest. Do you like your chili with rice or pasta or toast?" she asked suddenly.

"Uh…"

"Sam likes rice."

"Then rice it is."

"Grated cheese on top?"

"Sure."

"And salad to start."

"I told you, you don't have to—"

"Let me," she answered him. "Please let me, Patrick."

He sensed that it was important to her, so he let her turn the simple dish into a terrific meal, poured soda for her and cracked a beer for himself, so he could stand in the kitchen with her and talk while they worked together. Hesitantly, she told him more about the reason for her stepsisters' trip to New York, then seemed relieved when he switched to lighter subjects.

It was so nice, he wished it could go on for hours, and he jumped when he heard Sam's voice calling from the other room, "Aunt Cattie?"

It was as if their cooking and talking had woven a cocoon around the room, and Sam's innocent voice had torn it open. When had he felt this way with a woman before? Ever? He fought back a sigh, sensing that his troubles had only just begun.

Sam went to bed at eight, and Patrick muttered something apologetic about work he needed to get done on the computer.

"If you need to go out for any reason, I don't mind listening out for him," he offered.

Cat shook her head. "Actually, I need to study," she told him. "I have a block of nursing practical work starting next week, and I brought some notes over from the house."

"Shall I put on some music? Will it distract you?"

"Not at all. I always have music on when I study. Usually Pixie's old radio, tuned to her favorite country station."

"Music coming up, then."

Cat held her breath, wondering what he would choose. Here in the living room, there was a very large sound system set up in a sleek, purpose-built cabinet, with some very loud amplifiers to match, and she half-expected to hear a heavy metal band, cranked up loud enough to shake the room.

Instead, the sound of mellow classical guitar began to trickle through the apartment. It wasn't something she'd ever listened to before in her life, but it was...wonderful, actually. Peaceful. Beautiful. Made it easy for each of them to focus on their work.

When he was safely seated in front of his computer in another room, she stealthily got her wire-framed reading glasses out of her purse, slipped them on and began her study of nursing care of the post-operative child.

She didn't know, a half hour later, how long he'd been standing in the doorway looking at her. But she did know, quite well, why her hand flew up instinctively to her glasses the moment she became aware of him.

Pure vanity! The same vanity that had made her put them on so stealthily before.

And it's ridiculous because I don't *want* his attraction. I should put in orange-peel teeth, like a Halloween witch, and not wash my hair for the next week, instead of trying to hide my glasses!

And why was he laughing?

She glared at him over the tops of the frames, then snatched them off and put them away in their case. Score one for vanity, zero for good sense.

"What?" she demanded.

He didn't answer, just kept laughing softly.

"No, I mean it," she insisted. "What is it? We didn't have spinach, so I can't have any stuck in my teeth."

"Just wondering how many different people you are, Cat Brown, that's all. And wondering when I'll get to meet one that I don't like."

"How many—?"

"Lady Catrina Willoughby-Brown came first, and I liked her a lot. She was pretty cluey, but a lot more vulnerable than she let on. Then came Miss Catrina the Swiss milkmaid at the rink two weeks ago."

"Milkmaid?"

"Yeah, with the blond braids and the clear, freshly scrubbed skin. *She* looked like she wouldn't say boo to a goose, but she sure had some strong opinions about fairy tales! She came as a bit of a shock, but I had to respect and admire her for her courage in stating what she believed."

"Wasn't courage. Just sense!"

He ignored her. "Since Saturday night, you've mostly been plain Aunt Cattie, playing all the great roles that mothers and aunts and grandparents have to play—cook and play-mate and hugging machine. Now, after all that, I suddenly find out that you wear glasses when you read, and you concentrate so hard on the..." He read carefully upside down. "*Nursing Care of Children and Families* that I can deliberately clear my throat three times to get your attention and you don't even hear. Want some coffee?"

"If it's decaf."

"Coming right up."

So he made coffee and they each worked for another hour, to the gardenia-scented sound of Billie Holiday on the sound system. And when she interrupted him, this time, to tell him she was going to bed, he idly asked her why she'd decided to become a nurse, and they ended up talking over more coffee, for almost another hour.

She found out about his seven brothers and his doctor dad and ex-nurse mom. They weren't the millionaire business people she'd assumed they would be, but decent, ordinary people who'd worked hard, used their brains and made good in life. She found out about his twin nieces Maggie and Rosie, and their parents Tom and Julie. She heard about his brother Adam, his daughter Amy and wife Meg, and Connor and his fiancée Allie and her little girl, Jane. All that family! All those successful, loving bonds.

And she told him more about herself. About her dad and his struggle. About Rose, and Jodie and Pixie and the trailer park. About the goals she and her sisters had, fears they shared, mistakes they'd made.

He asked who had come up with the idea for gate-crashing the ball, and she told him about Jill coming across several blank invitations at the rink.

"Powerful things can happen at fancy balls," Jill had announced darkly, holding the invitations up like a winner's trophy. "Let's see if we can make the glamour work in our favor for once."

"Make it work?" Patrick echoed when Cat described the scene. "Lady C, you molded the glamour like clay in your hands."

They laughed about it.

It was worse than if he'd tried to seduce her. Much worse! Dear lord, on top of everything else she reluctantly felt about him, they were becoming *friends!*

Jill came back from New York the next day, alone.

"Suzanne has found a friend's couch to sleep on," she told her stepsister. "I don't know how long she's planning to stay. A while, I expect. She wants that baby, Cat!"

"I thought she might. Do you think she has a chance?"

"Of getting custody?" Jill shrugged and sighed. "At the moment, there seems to be no one else, but mom's taking the train up tomorrow, with that creepy new boyfriend of hers."

Neither Cat nor Jill pursued this subject. They each had as little as possible to do with Rose Brown these days. That was the way it had been for five years or more, and Rose had given them no reason to change their attitude.

Suzanne was the only one who still found favor with Rose, and that was only because of Suzanne's innate generosity in the way she responded to her cold-hearted mother's demands. This was how she'd first learned that Rose had put a baby girl up for adoption at seventeen. Suzanne had been nursing Rose after the latter's face-lift surgery in April, when Jodie had called out of the blue in search of her birth mother.

Rose had repudiated any thought of meeting her thirty-seven-year-old daughter, so Jodie had met Suzanne instead and the two of them had connected warmly at once. At a later meeting, Jill had also warmed to Jodie, and they all knew the broad details of her life now.

Her adoptive parents had died late last year, impelling her to seek her birth mother. She had been happy and secure in her career as a pediatrician. She hadn't found love in her life, but had decided to opt for single parenthood and was happily pregnant through artificial insemination, despite the fact that some people didn't approve of her choice in this area.

"Suzanne is the right person to raise Alice," Jill told Cat, echoing Cat's own feeling on the issue. "I know she is! But I have a sense that it's not going to be as easy to arrange as she hopes."

As she spoke, she distractedly unpacked a small suitcase in the room at Patrick's that she was going to share with Sam for the next few days. Sam was at preschool summer day camp this morning until lunchtime. Jill had driven back early. Miraculously, the Buick had performed as it was supposed to. Now, she was on her way to see the house.

"I still can't take it all in," she said. "They really think the fire was deliberately set?"

"I had to talk to the arson squad yesterday morning," Cat confirmed. "They don't seem to be in any doubt. They're still working on tracing the owner of the car."

"And I can't work out why we're staying *here!*"

She fixed Cat with an expression that said, "Tell it to me straight!" and as usual Cat couldn't fudge the truth to the stepsister who could nearly have been her twin.

"I can't believe it, either," she admitted. "He was just *there*. I didn't even question it at first... I practically fell on top of him."

Into his arms. Against his mouth. She didn't admit to this part of it.

"He saved Pixie's life, Jill, and since then he's been..."

"Coming on to you like an animal in heat, right? Calling in the favors you owe?"

"Actually, no..."

"No? Then he's the patient type. Biding his time."

Cat hid the twist in her guts that Jill's take on the situation instantly produced.

Was that really Patrick's attitude? His only motivation? Maybe it was. Probably it was. Just three days ago...less...she'd have thought exactly the same thing herself. Now, she didn't want to admit to Jill or even to herself how much she'd started to hope that Patrick Callahan was different.

"Since when did you get so cynical, Jill Brown?" she answered lightly.

"Oh, you know me, cynical's my middle name."

Yeah, and I used to think it was mine....

"Let's get going, if you want to see the house," she said. "Or we won't make it back to Sam's preschool by twelve-thirty."

Okay, not subtle enough.

"Changing the subject?" Jill teased.

"Respect that!" Cat retorted.

"We can talk about me instead, if you like."

"Great idea. What's new?"

Unexpectedly, Jill flushed and frowned and twisted her fingers together. "A proposal, Cat. That's what's new. Alan asked me to marry him."

"Jill—"

"Over the phone, when I called from New York."

"But you've only been out with him three times!"

"It's a practical kind of thing." Jill threw the words over her shoulder as she picked up her purse. "We didn't need a lot of time. It's not about love." Suddenly the casual facade dropped and her tone grew intense and emotional. "Sam doesn't need that, Cattie. He doesn't need a mom who's so starry-eyed with what she wants to believe is love that she can't see straight.''

"I guess not…"

"He doesn't need me scanning the horizon for a knight in shining armor so that I don't even see what's on my own doorstep. Sam needs me to find a good, solid, stable man who's got something to give to the partnership and who's going to get something out of it in return. That's what it's about…"

"I'm not arguing, Jill."

Had she heard?

"…Security, and putting the kids first. Alan is here, right now, and that's what he's offering."

They took the elevator down to the underground parking garage, where Patrick had arranged guest parking for the ancient Buick.

"So you said yes?" Cat questioned on the way. She thought she was stating the obvious, but apparently not.

"Uh…" Jill flushed more darkly "…no…"

"You said no? After that speech you just gave me about—"

"Not that, either."

"I don't get it, Jill."

"I want to say yes. I told him that. But there's something I have to deal with first."

"Okay…"

"I'll keep you posted."

"You do that. Because I'm interested. Your whole take on knights in shining armor is…uh… interesting." Her turn to flush, now.

Jill threw her a shrewd look and nodded silently. Then they let the whole subject drop. For some reason, for both of them, it was a little dangerous right now. Instead, they looked at the house, talked to the work crew, shuddered at the devastation in the hallway.

"We've had to rip more stuff out before we could start building it back up," said Bill, the crew's boss. "It'll start looking better by the weekend."

"We're hoping to move back in," Jill said.

"Fine, if you don't mind hammering at seven in the morning."

They took some smoke-stained clothing to launder at Patrick's, then picked up Sam, had sandwiches in the playground and went to visit Pixie. Jill was working at the rink after this, from four in the afternoon until it closed for the night. She took Sam with her, to stay until his bedtime, as he loved to skitter around on his little hockey skates, or play with a box of toys in the office. Cat would pick him up later.

Meanwhile, Cat went back to Patrick's and did the laundry, putting each load through the machine twice before it lost the smell of smoke.

Patrick arrived home just as she was putting the second load into the dryer.

"Since you're on a roll with the household chores, want to come grocery shopping?" he said.

"This is to feed your houseguests, right?"

"Right. So it would be very impolite of you to refuse. Impolite and unwise, because I don't know much about what you guys eat."

Cat had never shopped this way before. To her, grocery shopping was a chore. You did it when you had to, when supplies were low and you could scrape together the cash. You took hours over it, because you had to compare prices obsessively and maximize coupon usage. By the time you left, you always had a headache, and you never had quite all you wanted, because the dollars just wouldn't stretch that far.

Patrick wasn't interested in shopping that way. He chose the pricey, exclusive and gorgeously laid out gourmet supermarket near his apartment building, which had exotic items on its shelves that Cat had only ever read about in books.

When he saw something that appealed to him, he put it in the cart. If it appealed a lot, he added more. And if he saw Cat eyeing an item with a light of hunger in her eyes, he put in a good half dozen.

Freshly made pizzas from the deli, covered in cling wrap. Hand-picked raspberries and premium ice cream. Sticks of French bread. Free-range eggs. The kind of cereal that was so good for you it practically walked out of the store on its own.

He teased her. "Go on, admit it, you want key lime pie for dessert."

"It's fine."

"You want it," he chanted. "You want it *bad.*"

"Do *you* want key lime pie for dessert, Patrick?"

"Ah, you twisted my arm again!" Two frozen pies went in the cart.

Avocadoes, English cheese, imported beer, pistachio nuts. Hot dogs and ketchup and peaches for Sam. Jill's favorite cookies. Pixie's preferred brand of soap. Pre-packed salad greens for Cat.

"*Stop,* Patrick," she demanded angrily, when they'd zigzagged through the store three times and the cart was full to overflowing. "Just *stop!*"

"Why?"

"Because we don't need all this."

"What's need got to do with it?"

"Believe me, a lot!"

He ignored her and threw in two jars of caviar. "We'll have this with a cocktail before dinner, or something."

"No!"

"Aw, Cat, I'm still having fun…"

She bracketed her hands on her hips, blocked half the aisle and almost yelled. "Well, I'm sorry, but I'm not here to provide amusement for—"

"Lady Catrina? Is it really you?"

The innocuous-looking gray-haired man who had been gradually overtaking them down the aisle suddenly did a double take and turned back to face them, and his features crystallized into those of none other than local Councillor Earl P. Wainwright.

Cat stopped cold in her tracks and her face fell. To the floor, it felt like. She picked it up quickly and put it back on. Ping! A dazzlingly regal and beautifully condescending smile set there like concrete. "Why, Councillor Wainwright!"

Unfortunately, with so little time to prepare, she forgot all about the accent, and he must have heard her yelling at Patrick in pure American, anyhow.

The councillor was looking first puzzled, then taken aback, and finally very ready to explode.

"Earl!" said Patrick, covering the frowning, red-faced councillor's hand with his in a hearty shake. "Uh, *Earl!*" he repeated more urgently, then dropped his voice to a conspiratorial hiss. "Don't open your mouth about this! Please! You see… uh…Lady Catrina doesn't want anyone to know she's still in Philly."

"She—"

"The accent's convincing, isn't it? A very effective form of disguise. You'd hardly suspect she wasn't a native. The occasional dropped *r* or shortened *a*, but I'm so proud of her."

He gave an enormous, goofy grin, like a lovelorn puppy, and whipped his arm around Cat's shoulders so fast she could barely keep her feet on the ground.

"You see," Patrick went on expansively, spreading his free arm wide. "The miraculous thing is...uh...we're engaged! That's why she's still in town."

"But didn't you only meet—?"

"Yes! At the ball! Just two and a half weeks ago. So you can see why we're keeping it a secret, and going to these lengths. Incognito's the word, isn't it? Her father would never approve of such an impulsive courtship. If he hears a word about this, if the British tabloid press get hold of it.... But of course as soon as we saw you, I realized we'd have to let you in on it."

"I see." Councillor Wainwright frowned again. "Incognito." Then his brow cleared. "Well, that's marvelous! Wait until I tell Mrs. Wainwright. She's away this week. So is the maid. Which is why I'm shopping." The frown was back. "And I can't find the hot dogs."

"Processed meats section. Aisle two," Patrick told him helpfully.

"Aisle two," the councillor nodded.

"Definitely aisle two," Patrick confirmed in an encouraging tone.

He still had an arm around Cat, stiff as an iron bar. Now he drew her even closer and snuffled his lips all the way up her neck, past her ear and around to her temple, as if he were hungry, and she tasted like dessert.

Cat squirmed. It tickled. This was evidently Patrick's view of how Earl P. Wainwright must have behaved as an ardent young lover, and evidently he was right. The councillor's beaming smile was back in place and now stretched from ear to ear.

"You wait until Mrs. Wainwright hears this!" he repeated. "You're a lucky man, Patrick Callahan, and I can see that you know it. Do call me this week and tell me more about that customized software program you think I should implement in my business, won't you? Seems to me it probably *is* just what I need, after all!"

"I'll do that, sir," Patrick said. "I'll certainly call with all the information you need."

He turned to Cat. "Darling, isn't that splendid!" he exclaimed. "The councillor is going to equip his business with Callahan Systems software!"

This time, his lips smacked happily against her cheek.

"Splendid!" Cat muttered as Earl Wainwright set off in search of the hot dogs in aisle two. She added a second later, "Patrick, I hate you!"

She wiped her cheek with the inside of her arm.

"You actually mean, 'Thank you from the bottom of my heart,' don't you?"

"No..." She sighed. "Yes! But couldn't you have thought of—?"

"In the quarter of a second remaining to me before the man had steam coming out of his ears, thinking he'd been tricked at the ball the other night? No, I could *not* have thought of a story that didn't involve body contact. What's wrong? You liked that part too much?''

"No, it tickled so much I had to practically bite my cheeks to keep from squirming.''

"Maybe I'd better do it properly, then. He's looking at us from the end of the aisle. And he's frowning again. Ready?''

"No!''

"Cat, just how much is your stubbornness worth to you?'' He gave a crooked grin. "I'm kissing you whether you like it or not!''

He leaned over her, menacing and utterly delicious, the way he smelled, the way he sounded, the way he looked.

Why is my entire body turning to Jell-O?

It hadn't done that just now when Patrick had been putting on a performance for Councillor Wainwright.

But this kiss was different. This time, Patrick paid full attention to what he was doing, took his time over it, behaved like his normal self, and did it properly.

He stood right in front of her and cupped his hands around her hips, spreading heat across her stomach, two waves of it, meeting in the middle. He dipped his head slowly, tilting it a little, then stopped just an inch shy of her mouth. He studied her lips, his lids half lowered over his blue eyes so that all she could see were his thick black lashes.

It seemed as if he was never going to touch her mouth, never consummate the moment, and she was on fire for it, going dizzy with anticipation and need, despite the part of her mind that clamored, "Pull away now, be strong, take a stand, don't let this happen. It's dangerous, and there's something about it that isn't right."

He scraped his teeth gently across the fullness of his bottom lip, as if still absorbed in solving a complex problem. Hmm... The best angle of attack, perhaps. The sight drew her gaze and made her own lips part involuntarily. She felt the rhythm of his breathing, deep and steady, though she knew her own breathing was fluttering in and out like that of a feverish child.

Then, at last, he moved one hand to the small of her back, pulled her against him and touched his lips to hers, like locking the final piece of a jigsaw puzzle into place. At once, a cascade of feeling poured through her.

"There!" he said, his mouth soft and sweet on hers. His hand trailed slowly up from her hip to brush her achingly sensitive breast and settle on her shoulder. His thighs pressed against hers, hot and hard. She gave a shudder. Almost whimpered aloud. "There..." he repeated, then parted his lips deliberately and deepened the kiss for a long, melting moment, before he pulled away.

He looked down at her, grinning, like the cat that got the cream. Confidence radiated from him like ultraviolet light. "That should about do it," he said, his voice as sure as silk.

Do it for who?

He glanced down to the end of the aisle, and Cat did the same. Councillor Wainwright had disappeared. Patrick shrugged as if the whole thing was unimportant, grinned again, and turned back to the shopping cart.

Cat was immediately, totally and utterly furious.

Chapter Eight

"It was just a kiss, Cat."

"No, it wasn't. And it's only half the issue. And don't you ever, ever kiss me like that again!"

Cat stalked ahead of Patrick out of the supermarket. It had taken them another half hour to finish their grocery shopping. This was partly because the checkouts were crowded, but mostly because Cat had insisted on going back down the aisles and replacing at least half of the items Patrick had so casually tossed into the cart.

"I don't know what this is about." He didn't try to hide his impatience and anger.

"Neither do I, but don't worry, I'll work it out."

"And you'll let me know, I suppose."

"Possibly."

"I won't hold my breath while I wait."

"If you feel like holding your breath, Patrick, please don't let me stop you!"

But he'd had enough. Patrick Callahan, CEO and

co-founder of Callahan Systems Software did *not* push shopping carts through supermarket parking lots loudly trading insults and accusations with women.

Not any women.

And most especially not women like Cat—*were* there any other women like Cat? he briefly wondered—who quite clearly did not belong in his life, and about the only concession he was prepared to make to her at the moment was his admission that *she* had been the one to point that out from the beginning.

She didn't belong in his life.

Maybe it was time he accepted her point.

Only problem was, she still needed him, and so did her family and he was too stubborn—and possibly too well-brought up by that maddening mother of his—to renege on the commitment he'd made to giving her a roof over her head until she and Jill and Sam and Pixie could return to their home.

He gritted his teeth. Four more days? Five? Six?

Sam was cute. So was Pixie. He could handle sharing his apartment with them, no problem. Jill seemed like a nice woman, if, like Cat, a little too cynical. Cat herself, on the other hand, was a painful thorn in his side. What was worse, she gave him an even more painful ache in his groin.

Since she was still walking ahead of him, apparently spitting mad, with her shoulders pressed proudly back, her head held high and her feet marching straight and fast, he was treated to the full truth about just how strong was his physical response to her.

Incredibly strong.

It made him ache, made him sweat, made things happen to his heart rate and his breathing that his doctor father Jim and doctor brother Adam might have had something to say about. It put him in a painfully bad mood and made him dizzy with high-octane energy, both at the same time.

So maybe that was all it was? He had the hots for her, to put it as crudely as possible. He was enthralled by her neat, youthful breasts, no doubt jutting enticingly and bouncing just the right amount as she stalked ahead of him. His hand itched to curve over that pert, peach-perfect rear end. He wanted to run his fingers through her hair, twist soft tendrils of it around his knuckle, lift the golden mass to kiss her neck and taste the sweetness of her skin.

Yep, it was the hots.

And that was all!

A man knew how to compartmentalize that aspect of his life, didn't he? He didn't have to let it affect his judgment in other areas. So, okay, it was settled and he felt better. The hots. He could deal with it.

"I was wondering," he heard himself say. "On the weekend, since you probably won't be back in your house…"

"Yes?"

"Rather than hang about in the hot city…" he envisaged Pixie wilting, Sam bored and Jill ill at ease "…want to come up to the mountains with me? Those keys my mom dropped off yesterday are for my brother's place, which is—"

She gave a short, hard laugh. "Okay, I was wondering when we'd get around to this."

"Get around to *what?*"

"Payback time. Bed, in payment for favors received. The answer is no, Patrick."

Cat turned deliberately and glared back at him. She had her hands on her hips and her shoulders still pressed back, which lifted her breasts inside the pink tank top she wore and sent such a stab of need shooting through Patrick that he almost confessed straight out that she was quite right to think the worst of him.

Yes, that's what I want. To take you off into a cabin in the woods and ravish you. As often as possible. In a wide range of different settings. At all hours of the day and night. I admit everything.

He understood the reason for her anger, now. Somehow, that sizzling, fabulous kiss they'd shared beside the ice-cream cabinet in aisle twelve had convinced her that sex was all he wanted. He still wasn't sure what the overly bountiful supply of groceries had to do with the problem—maybe she didn't know, either—but he would ignore that bit for the moment.

He'd focus, instead, on the sex thing.

"That's not what I meant," he told her, still wishing it was exactly, and only, what he'd meant.

"No?"

"No!"

He stopped, groping for honesty. Since he didn't seem to be able to experience any consistent feeling about Cat Brown for more than thirty seconds at a stretch, honesty was a little difficult to achieve, but he gave it his best shot.

He took a deep breath and clarified, "*Most* of the time, it's not what I mean. Occasionally, I admit, all I can think of is—" He stopped again. "But I guess that's *my* problem. The point, at the moment, is that when I talked about the weekend, I meant that Jill and Sam and Pixie were invited as well."

"You did?"

"I did. You know, to give you all something to do. A bit of a break. Which would tend to make wall-to-wall seduction a little difficult for me to achieve, don't you think?

"Uh, yes, well, then, that's nice of you—"

"Damn it, it isn't *nice* of me!" he retorted, seething with frustration. "None of this is me being nice. Not really. It's more like a set of dominoes falling.... I don't know what it is. All I know is that I couldn't get you out of my head after the ball, which ended up putting me on the spot when your place got torched, which meant you had to come and stay, and that has so far proved to be a lot more fun than I'd ever have imagined. Now you're making these accusations, and to be honest, Cat, there's a part of me that wants them to be true."

"That doesn't make sense."

"My mother could tell you, and my brothers, that with my track record with women, only wanting sex would be a darn sight more familiar and more convenient than wanting all the baggage that goes with it. Especially in your case."

They reached the car and he made it whoop as he unlocked it by remote. She had a crackling paper grocery bag out of the cart and into her arms before he'd even opened the trunk, and as she placed it inside she muttered, "That's what I thought. That's exactly what I thought."

"And since for some reason I haven't worked out yet—there's a lot of things I haven't worked out yet in relation to you, apparently—you're not the kind of woman I'm only going to have sex with..."

"Because I'm not a woman that *any* man only gets to have sex with," she pointed out.

"That," he agreed. "Other reasons, too. Don't make the mistake of thinking it's only coming from you, Cat. Sheesh, I've lost my train of thought completely, now!"

"We'll come to the mountains, okay?" She had a hunted look on her face. "Is that what you want me to say? Sam will love it. It'll be a huge treat for him. And—and maybe we all need to get away after all that's happened lately. Is it a big place?"

"Yeah, on its own island."

"So maybe you'll hardly have to see us if you don't want to, and when the weekend is over, we can move back to our place and get out of your life."

Cat expected him to argue, but he didn't. Instead, they packed all the groceries into the trunk and drove back to his place in silence.

Catrina hardly saw Patrick over the next three days. He was busy at his work and came home late Wednesday and Thursday nights.

Even at ten at night, business-related phone calls chased him. Once or twice, Cat heard his voice raised through his study door and had the impression that there were issues developing between him and his brothers that he couldn't manage to resolve.

She came so close to knocking on his door and going in to ask if there was anything he needed, any way she could help. Maybe get him a coffee or a cool drink, run him a bath, rent him a video comedy.

She remembered that other night when they'd talked, and knew, deep down, that she was angling for a repeat of that unthreatening closeness.

But in the end, she stayed away. She was too unsure about how he'd interpret her concern, and too unsure, herself, about what it meant. Better to focus on Jill and Pixie and Sam instead, because they were three out of the four people who really counted in her life, and with them she truly knew where she stood.

Knowing how emotionally fragile her cousin could be, she didn't let Pixie visit the burned-out house until Friday. By then, the fire-damaged materials had all been removed, leaving gaping expanses ready to rebuild. A team of cleaners had done considerable work on the smoke-damaged bedrooms, but Pixie still cried and wrung her hands at the scorched window frames, the yellowed walls and lingering smell.

It took a visit to Giselle, still at Joan Mark's house next door, to cheer her up.

"The moment the gas is back on, we're moving in," she told Giselle, as seriously as if Giselle could understand.

And perhaps she could. She yapped and wagged her tail, and when Pixie kissed her, she practically kissed back.

At four in the afternoon, they left Pennsylvania in Patrick's luxury sedan, tooled up the New Jersey Turnpike, then crossed into New York State to I-87, bypassed the city of Albany and reached the seclusion of Diamond Lake just after dark.

Sam was thrilled by the boat ride across to the

island, and then thrilled by everything else about the entire weekend. Pixie spent almost the whole time lolling in a hammock strung between two pines, enjoying the summer breeze off the water. Jill and Sam swam and paddled a canoe crookedly around the lake.

Cat alternated between looking after everyone to an unnecessary degree and lazing in the shade with a book, taking more notice of Patrick than she was prepared to admit, even to herself.

So he had a great body in swim shorts, and could swim all the way out to the rocks in the middle of the lake and back again without having to quicken his breathing? So he taught Sam how to fish and how to find frogs and painted turtles, and where a patch of blueberry bushes grew, ripe with dusky fruit? So he managed to produce great meals, like bagels and cream cheese and fresh coffee for breakfast, and crisply heated pizza for dinner, without apparently spending more than five minutes at a stretch in the kitchen? So what!

And if their eyes kept meeting whenever they were in the same room, and if they kept laughing at the same things, and if both of them scored a hole-in-one on the same hole at the mini-golf course in the nearby town of Lake Edward where they went for some entertainment on Saturday night—Patrick won, of course—well, all that was even less significant.

Cat got back to Pennsylvania on Sunday night hating Patrick for getting her confused like this. She didn't know which way was up. She sincerely wished, fifty percent of the time, that they'd never met. The other fifty percent of the time, she didn't have the slightest idea how she was going to manage to forget him.

"Gas is going on for sure, definitely, first thing tomorrow morning, Cat," Jill announced over dinner Monday night.

"That's great!" she answered.

She had started her block of nursing practical today and was more tired than she wanted to be after a day of nursing children who'd just come out of surgery or were about to undergo it.

"Isn't it?" Pixie agreed. "And isn't it lucky I made my cake tonight?"

She had worked on the mocha chocolate mousse cake for hours and it was gorgeous. If the huge slice that had already nearly disappeared into Patrick's mouth was any guide, he appreciated it to its full value. He cut himself a second slice, almost as large, muttering something about heaven on a plate.

"Hey, Callahan! Is that the kind of example you set for my son?" Jill teased him, pointing at the second piece.

Cat winced. Over the past couple of days, Jill had fallen into the most appalling habit of teasing the man, as if she felt totally at home with him and liked him hugely. Well, theoretically that was good, Cat amended mentally. Of course it was! She hardly wanted the two of them to be tense with each other.

But this brother-and-sister act made her very uncomfortable, and she was tempted to take her sister aside and order, "Lay off! We're leaving tomorrow. He'll make a couple of token enquiries about how we're doing over the next couple of weeks. We'll pay him back for every cent he's spent on us as soon as the insurance check comes through, and then he'll be out of our lives.''

And that's what I want! she told herself firmly. Because that's the easiest way. To think that anything else is possible is just kidding myself.

Patrick laughed at Jill's jibe, then his face fell back into the preoccupied, frowning expression it had worn since he got home tonight. More tensions at work? Cat wondered.

He disappeared into his study right after his third piece of cake. Cat cleared up, then found that Sam and Pixie were both in bed and Jill was catching up on TV. Television didn't appeal to her. She needed something more active to distract her so that later her mind would slow enough for sleep.

There was a gym and racquetball club in the building, complete with pool and hot tub, and Patrick had obtained guest passes for her and Jill to use. She'd been down there several times now. Twice, she'd met Patrick coming out of the racquetball courts after a game. Each time, he'd looked sweaty and satisfied, while his opponent wore a chastened expression and was panting like a steam train. It had been such a telling and typical sight that she'd had to laugh, and Patrick had of course demanded to know why.

She hadn't told him.

Tonight, he seemed safely absorbed in his work, so Cat took her jaunty one-piece swimsuit, told Jill where she was going and went down, with the goal of completing at least fifty lengths of the twenty-five-yard pool before bed.

The place was quiet tonight, and it was peaceful and physically satisfying to churn up and down the pool in her brightly patterned suit of neon orange, yellow and pink.

Peaceful, that is, until Patrick arrived and they caught sight of each other as she rested for a few moments at the end of her lane between laps. His expression told her clearly that he hadn't known she was here, so she resisted the temptation to accuse him of following her.

He dropped a towel onto one of the lounging chairs, which skirted the pool, said, "Hi," and dove in, and she couldn't help turning to watch him as he powered through the water in his black swim trunks, away to the far end then back again.

"Are you leaving?" he asked a few minutes later, grabbing the lane rope that separated them.

"Not yet," she answered. "Ten more laps, then I'm going to take a turn in the hot tub."

He nodded, then began to swim again, and she completed her fifty, got out and went over to the hot tub a short distance away. He couldn't have swum more than fifteen lengths himself before he joined her in the hot, churning water.

"So you're going back to the house tomorrow?" It sounded like a challenge.

"Are you counting the hours?" she retorted right back.

"You know I'm not."

"I don't know anything, Patrick," she said, suddenly tired to the bone.

Tired of feeling her attraction to him, and of fighting it. Tired of pretending to everyone—Pixie, Jill, Patrick—that he *didn't* make her senses swim every time she saw him. Tired of wondering just how con-

scious he was of the true depth of the effect he had
on her.

She pulled herself from the spa, dripping wet and
steaming, her hair running with water down the middle of her back and her swimsuit clinging tightly to
her body.

"Well, I'll tell you, shall I?" he said, hauling
himself out after her and grabbing her hand. "Tell
it the way I see it. I want to see you again. I don't
want to think that this is the end."

She sighed, and ran her hand down his wet, hard
arm to shake off his touch. "I guess you haven't got
what you came for yet."

"Ah, hell, are we back to that?" He wheeled
around in frustration, then turned back to her, blue
eyes blazing.

"Since that's the problem, yes!" she snapped.
Was it? In truth, she was just accusing him blindly,
in sheer self-defense.

She began to walk rapidly toward the change
rooms across the wet matting that surrounded the
pool. The attendant at the front looked at her for a
moment, then went back to his paperback.

"Tell me, Catrina Brown," Patrick demanded,
loping after her, "Hasn't it occurred to you that, for
a man who only wants one thing, I'm showing an
awful lot of patience about not getting it?"

"Is it patience, or is it not knowing your own
mind, Patrick?" She stopped and faced him just outside the change rooms, where a pillar and a potted
palm took them out of the pool attendant's view.
"I've had the impression more than once that you
didn't even know if you wanted a casual affair, let
alone anything else. You've said as much, haven't

you? And since I hope I haven't encouraged you to think I'm open to any of the options you might have in mind, no, I'm not surprised that you've 'shown patience,' as you put it.''

"None of the options?'' Patrick repeated, so frustrated he could hardly get out the words. She looked so cool and self-contained, standing there on the wet black mat in her colorful, dripping swimsuit. He ached for her. "None, Cat?''

Hell, he'd tried so hard over the past five or six days, since their blow-up outside the supermarket. He'd held himself back, hadn't come on to her, had simply tried to get to know Cat and her family, to be there for them, in the hope that what he and Cat each wanted, and what they each were capable of, would get clearer.

He'd thought they'd found a real connection, something to build on, and now she was denying everything. She had her arms folded across her chest, body language that shouted her defensive, impossible attitude. The gesture tightened the neat valley between her breasts. Droplets of water ran down and lost themselves there, and he could have licked each one away and not cared about the chlorine.

Oh, lord, and her lashes were wet and so were her lips, her hair was slicked back and darkened with water, leaving her face bare, clear of any shadow, any possibility of disguise. And in that moment he knew that she was the truest and most courageous woman he'd ever met.

Knew, too, that he wasn't going to let her go without the fight of his life.

"What about marriage?'' he demanded.

"Marriage?''

"Yes, damn it! Marry me!" He gripped her upper arms and pulled their wet bodies together, touching her thighs with his, feeling tiny goose bumps begin to rise on her skin. "That's what I want," he said. "If that's what it'll take to prove to you that I'm not looking to pick you up for some quick sex then toss you aside like a peach pit or something, then I'll do it. I'll propose. There you go! Marry me, Catrina Brown, and see how you like it!"

"No!" She laughed, a short, harsh sound. "No way, Patrick! Mercy on us, what sort of a proposal is that?"

"A real one. I'm not kidding, Catrina."

"Then you're crazy."

He grinned, sensing...quite certain that he sensed...her softening. "It's a good feeling."

His tone caressed her, and he watched her mouth, impatient for the moment when he could kiss the heat back into those cool, wet lips. "I think I've been more than a little crazy since the moment we met."

He brushed his mouth across hers, tasted the wetness and the chlorine as well as the familiar sweetness of her. He was dizzy with the sudden certainty that this was absolutely right, that he should marry this woman and spend the rest of their lives proving to her that none of her scruples and her suspicions mattered. Spend the rest of their lives happily getting her to admit that she was wrong.

But after just a second in which he felt her lower lip tremble beneath his, she pressed her mouth tightly closed and turned her head to the side, showing the smooth column of muscle at the side of her neck that he immediately wanted to kiss.

"I'm not going to marry you, Patrick," she said. "No matter who's crazy and who's not."

"Was this too sudden? Too informal, maybe?" he demanded. "Did you want candles and flowers? I can do all that. I can whisk you off for a weekend in Paris, and we can window-shop for a ring in the jewelry stores in the Place Vendôme."

"No! Damn it! Why are you saying this? Think about it, Patrick!"

"Hell, I'm saying it to prove to you—"

"Exactly!" she cut in. "You're saying it to win." She fixed him with her warm brown eyes, which were glittering with emotion and full of anger. "You're only saying it so you can win the game."

"You *feel* something." He instinctively knew he wasn't wrong. "You feel as much as I do!"

"I don't know what I feel. That doesn't matter."

"Of course it matters!"

"All I know is that this isn't about winning," she told him. "And you can't see that, can you?" She shook her head slowly. "Because this is the first time in your life it's ever happened to you, isn't it? The first time you haven't been able to get what you want. And if *that* doesn't convince you that we come from different worlds, I don't know what will, because I've spent my whole life fighting for things and not getting them, going after the impossible and having it stay just that—impossible."

"Cat—"

"Fighting and *losing*, Patrick. Fighting to build my father's faith in himself when he was stuck in a miserable marriage, fighting to win my stepmother's love, fighting to get our heads a little higher above water when we were kicked out of our home. Failing at all of that. Losing. Not getting what I want. It happens to other people all the time. Now it's happening to you.''

''No, Cat, you don't—''

He grabbed at her hand, tried to pry it out from where it was wedged between her upper arm and the side of her suit, but she shook him off.

''Don't act as if it's all so urgent,'' she said. ''I promise you, from experience, you'll have plenty of time to work out whether or not this particular failure matters. Welcome to the world!''

''Hell, no, Cat, you are the last person in the world I'd ever think of as failing,'' he insisted. ''Achieving what you have, I—''

''No, Patrick!''

She hadn't even stayed to listen. Feeling like he was burning, he watched as she snatched herself away from him and ran across the matting to the women's change room, her hands pressed to her ears to shut out his words.

He thought about waiting for her, saying it differently, arguing, kissing her until she was blind with wanting him and unable to say anything but, ''Yes.''

He knew she felt the chemistry, as hot and strong as he did. She was a sensual, passionate woman who had needs that left her vulnerable. He knew he could win something from her that way. Eventually. Even if it was just her body in his bed for a few short nights. That would be a victory in most men's eyes.

Then he thought of the passion in her face, the anger, the conviction, the sincerity and the vision, and a thread of doubt—or was it an upside-down kind of faith?—began to unravel inside him.

Could she possibly be right? Could she? Was that, after all, the only thing he had truly wanted from their fraught relationship? The only thing he wanted from that crazy, spur-of-the-moment proposal, as well?

To win?

Chapter Nine

"Do you think he'd marry me instead?" Suzanne asked, hugging her arms around her knees on Pixie's old couch.

As usual her tone was so deceptively mild that it took both Cat and Jill several seconds to notice the wicked gleam of humor in her green eyes. Then both sisters answered at once.

"Probably," said Jill.

"I doubt it," said Cat.

At this, all three of them did a double take and burst out laughing.

"Uh...who were you talking about, Suzanne?" Cat asked cautiously.

"Anybody," Suzanne answered simply.

She had returned to Pixie's to pack her things for a long-term move to New York City. Baby Alice was in New York, as well as Alice's doctors and Michael Feldman, Jodie's former partner in her pediatric practice. Dr. Feldman was the executor of

Jodie's will and Alice's temporary guardian. Determined to center her life around the baby if she possibly could, Suzanne's move was part of a future bid for permanent custody.

"Patrick Callahan, Alan Jennings," she went on. "I'd marry pretty much anybody right now. I can't believe that *both* of you have had marriage proposals in the past couple of weeks, and I'm the one that really wants one. You turned yours down flat, Cattie, and, Jill, you don't seem exactly over the moon about Allan begging for your final answer three times a day."

Her laughter was a little shaky now, and her liquid voice was strained. Underneath the teasing, she was deeply serious. Suzanne had always had such a warm, loving heart. If she lost baby Alice, they'd all have to help her pick up the pieces of her life and move on.

"Well, it's not that," Jill said reluctantly. "I mean, I want to say yes to Alan. Absolutely. It's just I..." She took a deep breath. "Well, it turns out I'm going to have to go out to Montana and get myself a divorce first."

"What?" Cat and Suzanne both shrieked at once.

"Is there a problem, girls?" Pixie cooed, poking her head into the old-fashioned sitting room.

She had been standing out in the hallway, chatting to the master woodworker who was finishing the new stair rail with period detail. Clyde Hammond wasn't proving all that fast on the job.

"Attention to detail is the hallmark of my work," he'd said solemnly, several times.

"Attention to Pixie is more like it," Jill had commented tartly, out of both his and Pixie's earshot.

Pixie's pink cheeks over the past few days gave a hint that the feeling was mutual, and there was a sense of hushed anticipation in the air. How did a wiry sixty-four-year-old carpenter with a slow, thoughtful way of talking ask a daffy sixty-two-year-old ex-ballet company wardrobe mistress for a date in the muddy waters of relationships in the new millenium?

At the moment, this question was less urgent than the ones Cat and Suzanne were throwing at Jill.

They deflected Pixie's attention with a soothing reply and she went back to her conversation with Clyde.

"A *divorce?*" Cat said.

"But you're not married! *Are* you?"

"*Who* are you married to?"

"When?"

"How?"

"*Why?*"

Jill blushed darkly.

"It's…really not important," she said. "This guy in Las Vegas…kind of saved me. You know that Cinderella Marriage Marathon contest thing that's been on TV? I was the so-called Celebrity Cinderella Bride, and he bid for me. We didn't know it was part of a contest, and that the marriage was real. We signed our way out of the contest, but we still need a legal divorce. I wrote to him about it last week, and I got an answer back yesterday saying he doesn't have time to think about it right now. And his phone number isn't in service anymore, according to the phone company, which means I can't call and push him on it, so I'm going to have to take Sam and go out there, is all."

She shrugged apologetically and chewed on her bottom lip. Cat had the distinct impression there was more to the whole thing than maybe even Jill herself understood.

"Right," said Suzanne faintly. "So not only have you recently received a perfectly serviceable proposal of marriage from one man, but you're also already married to someone else."

"That's correct. For the moment. As I said, it's not important. I'll have it dealt with in a month or so when I can get time off work, but until then I can't say yes to Alan and he understands that." She splayed her hands against her dark head. "Thank goodness! Because it's really—"

"Not important. Okay, we get the picture," Suzanne said, with a sarcastic bite to her tone that was unusual. "Cat, there's no chance Patrick Callahan would be interested in a substitute Brown sister?"

"Ah, Suze," Cat sighed, spreading her hands, "I don't think he's truly interested in the original Brown sister. It was just a game for him. It was about winning, that's all."

"Winning is good," Suzanne said. "If he married me, he could win a baby, too. The cutest little baby that's growing as fast as she knows how. *Too* fast, maybe. She'll be discharged pretty soon, so I don't have all that much time to make my case. I want to be the one to take her home from the hospital. And mom has found out that Alice will have Jodie's money—which I only just found out about myself—and now mom is saying she wants Alice, and since she's about to marry that creepy guy she's been going out with...."

She trailed off and brushed impatiently at some tears with the heel of her hand.

"You all think I'm too soft on mom," she went on, "But believe me I know her better than any of you. I know what she's capable of, and what her priorities are, and *she can't have that child.*"

Cat got up restlessly and began to pace the room. She didn't have the answers. Not any of them. The problems they each faced dragged her back to that night two weeks ago by the pool in Patrick's apartment building and reminded her of what she'd ended up telling him then.

Sometimes, in the real world, you didn't win. It was quite simple.

Catrina hadn't heard from Patrick since he'd helped them move back into the house. Afterwards, he had said goodbye and wished all of them good luck for the future. There had been a finality to his tone that was unmistakable.

"So I guess I *did* win that one," Cat thought to herself. "Since I was the one who said we shouldn't see each other again."

She hadn't known a victory could taste so much like a defeat.

"We have a problem," he told her on the phone eight days later.

When he explained the situation, however, she had to disagree.

"You mean *we* have a problem. Pixie and the Browns. Not you, Patrick."

"Okay, I'm not part of the problem, but I'm part of the solution."

"Only if I let you be."

"Ah, come on, Cat! Who is it that's only thinking about winning, now? Isn't that going a little far for a very small victory?"

This silenced her, because she knew straight away he was right. The council vote on the rezoning was next week. This week, this coming Saturday, Earl Wainwright had invited Patrick "and that marvelous fiancée of yours" to a barbecue to celebrate Callahan Systems' new business relationship with Wainwright Packaging Industries.

"There was a kind of question mark in his tone as he said it," Patrick reported to Cat. "Something tells me he's got doubts about you. Maybe we weren't quite as sharp and fast as we thought that day at the supermarket. I didn't think you'd want to blow it now, when you'd done so well at the Mirabeau Ball. I kind of hedged our bets, though. Told him I wasn't sure if you'd be in town, that you might be flying to London for your mother's fifty-third birthday."

The deep, familiar notes of his voice seemed to caress her over the cordless phone, and she found that she was curling herself tighter and snuggling down deeper on the couch, as if he was here with her and they were in each other's arms. It wasn't the way she wanted to react to him, but she couldn't seem to help it.

"My mother?" she echoed, trying to focus.

"Yes, your mother Lady Hester," he explained. "You see, your father, Lord Randolph, is...uh... throwing a small, exclusive party for her at the Ritz."

"Oh, *great!*"

"I was inspired to great flights of imagination by the example you provided at the ball, Cinderella."

"Can I ask you a favor?"

"Sure."

"Next time, don't."

"Hey, I think I did pretty good on the spur of the moment. When he called, I had no idea he was going to issue the invitation."

"Now I'll have to remember all those details. How old did you say she was?"

"Fifty-three. And I...uh...may have mentioned your brother as well."

"*May* have?"

"Well, I did. Sir Rupert. But I'm not sure if Earl was listening at that point. I admit, I got carried away."

Cat caught herself smiling helplessly into the phone. She stopped instantly and bit her lip instead. Then she sighed. "Okay, I guess we've got to do it, then."

"I'll pick you up at seven."

"And do I wear the Willoughby-Brown family tiara?"

"Featuring the famous Montgomery diamond?"

"Yes, that one. Not the other Willoughby-Brown family tiara featuring the cubic zirconia from the close-out sale at the local jewelry store," she commented sarcastically, earning his laugh.

This pleased her more than it should. Why did she get a little kick of pleasure and happiness inside her just because she'd managed to make the man laugh?

"No, no tiaras required," Patrick told her. "He said casual."

Casual? What was *that?* Cat had to wonder over the next two days.

Pixie went into a flutter and rushed off to the fabric store, returning with yards of linen look-alike fabric in a sort of beige shade, which she insisted on calling "ecru." She also insisted on making it into a trouser-suit and teaming it with extremely high-heeled and flimsy ecru sandals, a very narrow belt, pearl drop earrings inherited from her grandmother, and a brand-new blouse made from a gorgeous old piece of cream silk she found in her fabric stash.

To Cat, all this did not spell "casual," but she accepted that it fitted "the role," and tried to remember that the role was all that counted.

Inside her heart and in the depths of her stomach, while Pixie fussed about, getting her ready two hours ahead of time on Saturday afternoon, something jumped and did a backflip every time she thought about Patrick.

I do not have feelings for him! I'm not prone to such self-destructive impulses! The only reason we are even seeing each other is because of that damned rezoning.

But when she heard his rap on the old-fashioned brass knocker, recently re-attached to Pixie's brand-new front door, she felt so nervous she could hardly swallow. When she saw him standing on the porch, rocking back and forth on his heels and giving her a lazy smile, her greeting was just a husky whisper.

What was a man like this doing in her life? Look at him! Navy pants and an open-necked matching shirt, fresh shave, dark hair silky clean, grin white and perfect. He didn't fit on this dusty porch in this dusty, dreamy, run-down old street.

And he knew it.

She could see it in the way his blue eyes narrowed suddenly, almost but not quite masking the brief flare of desire he'd felt on first seeing her. It was all so clear to her.

Sure he still wanted her, despite his best judgment. Just the way she wanted him. The chemistry between them had existed from the very beginning. It had been enough to compel him to seek her out at the ball and afterwards offer shelter to her family; even issue her a rapid-fire marriage proposal—a marriage proposal that was about as loving and tender and need-filled as an ace served at match point in a professional tennis tournament.

But he was seeing things differently now, it seemed. He'd gotten the thing under control. He'd set the boundaries to his own satisfaction. He could look but not touch. Want but not need.

"You look perfect," he told her in a cool tone. "Pixie make that, did she?"

"Yes, she insisted I needed made-to-measure."

"Well, she knows her stuff. It fits like a kid glove. And here's a prop for you."

"I don't—"

"A ring," he explained, holding it out. It swung gently on the end of his forefinger, and he already had its little black velvet box back in his pocket.

"It's gorgeous!" She eyed the champagne solitaire diamond in awe. "But—"

"Borrowed it from my sister-in-law," he explained.

He slipped it on, his fingers light and warm

against her hand. He didn't prolong the touch, didn't turn it into an excuse for a caress, but her hand tingled all the same, and her breathing went funny and she hated herself.

"There!" he said. "You look cool, elegant, totally appropriate and definitely engaged."

"Thank you," she responded brightly, hiding her hurt and jeering at herself.

Appropriate. Just what a man whispered, his voice breaking with emotion, to the woman he loved, right? "Sweetheart, you look so appropriate!"

But after all, what do you want from the poor man? she thought. You were the one who said no to him. Now that he's realized you were right, you suddenly want him to change his mind and fall at your feet? No! *No!*

"You think I can carry it off, then?" she added as cheerfully as she could.

"You did it before, didn't you?"

"That was at night, at a big gathering, full of music and noise and people. This is going to be quieter, isn't it? Not so many places to hide. I'm nervous."

And it has nothing to do with what *you're* doing to me, Patrick Callahan!

"Hey..." he said softly. "Don't be. I meant it, before. You look perfect. And I'm not talking about the clothes."

Her breath caught in her throat yet again, and she had to frantically blink back tears and think of dog food, tax returns and root canal before she was in control enough to speak, and even then the words were filtered through her need to hide her heart from him.

"You surprise me sometimes, Patrick," she said, as cool as Lady Catrina herself might have been, had she really existed.

"Yeah?" he answered.

"You have this sort of...gratuitous streak of kindness in you."

He laughed at the way she'd expressed it. "Do I?"

"Yes. When a lot of men in your position wouldn't."

"No?"

"No."

He looked across at her as they walked to his car, parked in Pixie's grass-grown driveway. There was a beat of silence. Then he scowled suddenly and swore.

"Of course," he said. "A man in my position. Successful, therefore not entirely human, right? More like a machine. Hell, do you realize that it actually hurts when you dismiss me that way? Of course you don't! Because a man in my position isn't supposed to be able to get hurt. He isn't supposed to have feelings at all."

He swore once more, under his breath, then strode ahead to open the door for her.

Cat was stricken at the way he had interpreted her words...then stricken again at the thought that he had a point. Had she been doing that? Stereotyping *both* of them? Leaping to preconceived conclusions? Not giving either of them a chance to be who they really were?

Something in the universe suddenly shifted, tilted,

changed. But she didn't have time right now to think about exactly what it was, nor what it meant, whether it was cause for celebration or sadness.

"I'm sorry," she apologized at last, as he started the engine. Her face was burning and her temples were tight. "I phrased that badly."

"No," he corrected her. His tone was cool and even. "You phrased it honestly. Let's cut the crud, Catrina. We know where we stand with each other now. Tonight is a business event for both of us. We'll play our parts as best we can, then it'll be done with. Once the vote on the rezoning takes place, I can let it slip to Earl that we broke our engagement. We realized it was just a short-lived physical thing, or whatever. I mean, as if he'd even *ask* about why. It's just not going to be a problem. So let's enjoy ourselves tonight, if we can."

"If!"

"Yes," he insisted. "We can. Because I'll tell you one thing about me being one of life's winners, Cat. I've been on the other side of that fence, too. There are plenty of times I've lost at things. Sports. Business contracts. Not the really important things, maybe, but they still count. And no one has ever accused me of being a sore loser!"

By Earl Wainwright's standards, the evening barbecue might have been intimate and casual, but it was still the kind of event that Catrina had never attended before. There were about thirty people present, grouped in loose, shifting clusters on a large, terraced slate patio that eased seamlessly into a gorgeous and expensively manicured garden of flower beds, lawns, shrubberies and hedges.

Councillor Wainwright made a great show of cooking the barbecue himself, complete with chef's hat, plastic barbecue apron and an armory of dangerous-looking flippers and forks and tongs. He was good at it, too, cracking hearty jokes and making the guests feel at ease. Cat had begun to genuinely like the man upon whom so much of her family's future depended.

Although Earl was the star of the show, however, the real work of supplying the marinated kebab sticks and spice-coated chicken wings, not to mention the steaks and burgers, salads, breads, drinks and everything else, was done by professional caterers, inconspicuously directed by Mrs. Wainwright.

Most of the guests were too snobbish or successful in their own right to admit to any open reverence for a member of the British nobility. They mostly chatted to Cat about their own trips to England and were so utterly uninterested in anything she might have to say that she was able to get by on the occasional, "Really?" and "You don't say!" and "How marvelous!"

There were a few people who weren't so easy to deal with. Two of them were Earl P. and his wife, Darlene, of course, who both gushed and enthused in a way that made up in warmth and sincerity for what they lacked in finesse. A third was Lauren Van Shuyler, an old friend and professional associate of Patrick's, who greeted Cat with a kiss and tears in her eyes.

"I was just thrilled when I heard Patrick was engaged," she told Cat, leading her away to the drinks table and pressing a second glass of champagne into her hand. "May I toast you?" She held up her glass and clinked it against Cat's.

Patrick had been seized by an associate of Councillor Wainwright's and was being attacked with a series of questions about the Internet and the future of dotcom stocks, so Cat had to play the charade alone, and she didn't feel comfortable. Pretty, dark-haired Lauren seemed so nice. Too nice to be tricked in this way.

"My dad has spent about three years, on and off, trying to get Patrick and me to fall for each other," she confided. "But we both knew from the start it was never going to work and we had some good laughs about it. I have to tell you, having you on the scene really takes the pressure off!"

Cat laughed, remembered to keep the accent in place just in time and said, "Does it?"

"Oh, yes…until my dad finds another candidate."

"Find a candidate of your own, someone you love, and it won't be a problem," Cat said. She hadn't expected a wealthy and successful female friend of Patrick's to be so easy to talk to. Another prejudice on her part? She put the question aside for the moment and focused on Lauren herself instead.

A woman like this couldn't be short of would-be lovers, she concluded. She was attractive, intelligent and apparently a very nice person.

With a broken heart? Cat suddenly wondered. There was a look on Lauren's face, now, sad and distant and bewildered, as if she'd experienced love and it had let her down in an unexpected way.

"Well…" she said. "I was engaged until a few months ago. But it's no good if it isn't the right man.'' She forced a laugh. ''Even my dad was relieved when I broke it off with Ben four days before the wedding.''

''It's not always easy to know your own heart, is it?'' Cat said inadequately.

''I thought I knew mine,'' Lauren confessed. ''I thought I'd found the one who was truly meant for me. I broke my engagement with Ben because I was so sure. But time passed. Lock disappeared. Never made contact. So it seems like I was wrong. It hurt. Which is crazy, when we were never really together.'' She gave a crooked smile. ''Makes me confess things to strangers, I'm sorry. But you have such a lovely warm smile, I felt as if you'd understand. I hope you and Patrick are very happy together.''

Cat opened her mouth to speak, although she didn't know what to say. ''I'm not really Lady Catrina Willoughby-Brown, and Patrick and I aren't really engaged,'' were the words that leaped to mind. Patrick's hand on her elbow stopped her just in time.

''Catrina, darling,'' he said. ''This is difficult, isn't it?'' He didn't wait for her to answer, just went on, ''Lauren, I'll call you, okay? Cat and I have more people to meet.''

He led her away, then muttered as soon as they were out of Lauren's hearing, ''You were going to confess, weren't you?''

''She seemed so sincere, I felt guilty.''

''She is, and so did I, but I told her I'd call her, and I'll tell her the truth then.''

''I'm glad,'' Cat said. She hesitated, then added, ''And you were right in what you said about stereotyping, earlier. I'd stereotyped her, too. I was surprised she was so nice, and I shouldn't have been.''

He didn't answer her directly, and she was disappointed.

Instead, he encouraged her, ''Just another hour and we can go home, and you'll never have to do this again, since the council meeting is next Wednesday. Meanwhile, let's pretend I'm spiriting you off to a quiet corner of the garden, and you can take a break from the accent for a bit.''

''Good, because my mouth was giving way at the hinges.''

''Apparently Mrs. Wainwright is an enthusiastic grower of alliums and has dozens of different varieties here in a special series of garden beds behind this hedge.''

''Alliums?''

''The onion and garlic family. And I fully intend to inspect every single one. Why don't we share the experience?''

So they studied alliums for twenty minutes in the fading summer light, and he came up with some appalling puns about Mrs. Wainwright's passion that had Cat groaning and giggling at the same time.

Finally, just as she was about to wander back to the lighted, slate-paved patio, he took her arm and said quietly, ''There's something I've been wanting to tell you, Cat.''

At once her heart began to pound, though she didn't quite know why. Was it purely his touch? Or the resonant hint of meaning in his tone. This wasn't going to be another bad joke about onions.

''Yes?'' she said, trying to stay cool.

''I'm moving to New York very soon.''

"Oh, I—" Since she hadn't known what to expect, it hardly made sense for her brain to clamor that she hadn't expected *this*. Words—sensible ones, anyway—refused to come.

"I'll be setting up an office of Callahan Systems there," he went on. "It—well, it makes sense. Tom broached the idea a few months ago, and both he and Connor want me to be the one to go. We have a lot of big clients in New York, and we want to build our business there even more."

"Why are you telling me this as if it matters to me?" she blurted out, her voice harsh as she tried to hide what she felt. "It doesn't, does it? It's not as if we were seeing each other."

"No," he agreed. "I guess I thought you'd be interested because it's part of my realization that you were right in what you said that night by the pool. When I asked you to marry me, I was only doing it to win. Just the way you said. And that's not a good enough reason, is it? Marriage is too important for that."

Cat nodded, looking up at him, her teeth clenched behind lips that were closed but steady. She didn't realize how close they were standing to each other until he reached out and touched her.

Touched her with just one finger, brushing it across her lips, over to her ear then very gently back along her jaw.

"We had some nice moments, though, didn't we?" he said. "It was real."

"Yes, it was," she managed to say.

"A connection. It's changed me, Cat. More than I'd have thought possible in so short a time. It's changed what I'll be looking for in the future."

"In New York?"

"In New York," he echoed. "Just wanted you to know that."

"I—I'm glad. It's changed me, too."

"Yeah?" he prompted her softly.

"I'm too proud, sometimes. Too unforgiving?" she suggested.

"So you still haven't forgiven that arrogant marriage proposal of mine?"

"Not quite," she agreed. "But that's my problem, and I'm working on it."

"Good luck, then," Patrick told her. He took her hand in his, almost without thinking about it. Her skin was warm and soft, and her fingers long and fine-boned against his. "Good luck with everything."

His brain felt woolly and the words were thick on his tongue. They were a formula, didn't fully make sense. Here he was, standing in the dark in a garden that smelled like garlic mayonnaise, stumbling through a parting with a woman who had touched him as no woman had ever touched him before.

A woman, what was more, who trembled when he brushed a finger against her face, and melted against him when he kissed her, and looked at him with huge brown eyes that swam with desire.

But that hadn't been enough, and he'd lost the battle.

This was the essence of what drove them apart. It hadn't been enough, and she'd forced him to see that. Again, it was something no woman—or man, for that matter—had ever got him to do before when it was a question of something truly important. To concede defeat, against the odds. To accept that his will and his wanting, his fight and his vision, could not prevail.

And she'd done it with such strength and grace. No manipulation. No game-playing. She saw things clearly, and she called them as she saw them. Lord, he respected her, the way he respected only a very few people in his world, and to a degree that he'd never respected any of the women he'd been involved with in the past.

And despite all the pain and frustration and powerless regret inside him, he wished her well. He wasn't even sure that she realized all this, despite what he'd tried to tell her earlier about not being a sore loser. He wasn't sure that she realized any of it. Did she understand quite what a profound sense of equality they had achieved? It was doubtful.

"Patrick, am I allowed to pay you back in some way?" she was saying. "Pixie's planning to make you another cake and have you over to some splendid sort of English tea. She's poring over her recipe books, and I suspect you've gotten onto her permanent cake list and you'll go on getting cakes from her at intervals for the rest of your life, but—"

"Still admiring my wife's alliums?" came a hearty voice out of the darkness. "Most people don't realize what pretty flowers onions have if you let 'em grow long enough."

Cat gasped and clapped her hands to her mouth as Earl Wainwright stepped out of the shadows behind the hedge that separated the allium garden from the flower beds and lawn on the other side.

"Earl!" Patrick said, with a mixture of heartiness and uneasiness.

In his mind, he heard Cat's last heartfelt words,

spoken in the uncompromising accent of a Philadelphia native.

"Oo-oops!" Councillor Wainwright said on a slow drawl. "Forgot the accent, there, didn't you, Miss Brown?"

There was a beat of strained silence. Patrick looked down and discovered that he still had Cat's hand in his. Instinctively, he held it tighter and put his other hand around her shoulder, turning her and drawing her close so that her hip bumped against him and her shoulder nestled against his chest. He felt a little shiver ripple through her.

Then the councillor laughed, his head thrown back and his face revealing innocent delight. "You two! Patrick Callahan, you have got yourself *the* cleverest and most resourceful woman I have met in a long time! I may have a naive kind of a soft spot for anyone with a title in front of their name, but I did not get to be the owner of an extremely successful packaging materials manufacturing company without a pretty good brain."

"H-how—?" Cat stammered.

"You had me right in the palm of your pretty little hand at the Mirabeau Ball, my dear," he answered. "And even when we bumped trolleys at Carluccio's Market that day. But when I met up with that damned Grindlay fellow last week at a business function, and we got to talking about the zoning business, he happened to mention these three conniving Brown sisters, including, in particular, a brown-eyed beauty named Catrina. Well, I made a few inquiries and soon arrived at the truth."

"You did?" Cat echoed, the fine skin around her eyes tight with strain.

For a simple, self-made man, Earl Wainwright was not at all easy to read right at this moment.

"I also heard about your cousin's fire."

"Yeah, we had a fire a few weeks ago," Cat said, nodding.

"Seems the police don't think it was a coincidence."

"No. But so far they've had trouble proving that. The car driven by the arsonist was found abandoned in a parking lot just yesterday, we've been told."

"Fortunately, myself, I'm not bothered too much by things like proof," the councillor confessed comfortably. "Now I've got you completely terrified, haven't I? And you deserve it for playing such a trick on my wife and me! But if you think I'd change my mind on the rezoning when my own research has convinced me it's not in the best interests of my local area, then you don't know me very well."

Patrick felt Cat's heart start to beat normally again, and her breathing resume its regular rhythm. She was still trembling a little, but then so was he. Happened, for some reason, every time they touched.

"However," the councillor continued, "there is one thing I will expect in return for my vote on council. A wedding invitation! You're a lucky and very attractive couple, and I just know you'll be happy together for a long time to come."

Following the councillor back to the party for dessert a few minutes later, neither Cat nor Patrick had the heart to disillusion him with the truth.

Chapter Ten

"How do I look, Cat, dear?" Pixie said.

Once more, she'd been sewing up a storm, this time for her sixth date with Clyde Hammond, her lean, laconic carpenter beau. She wore a shell-pink summer frock with hand-stitched beading at the neckline for the Sunday evening outing.

"You look dainty and pretty and perfect," Cat told her truthfully. She kissed her cousin and was enveloped in her sweet, floral scent.

Clyde arrived a few minutes later. He looked like a skinny version of Clint Eastwood, and invariably treated Pixie with a slow, old-fashioned kind of courtesy that almost brought tears to Cat's eyes. Her fingers ached from crossing them in her fervent hope that things would work out between Pixie and Clyde.

After enjoying a long, cool drink on the front porch, the two elderly lovers went off to their movie, leaving Cat alone in the house. She was alone too often these days, and didn't like it, despite everything she had to be grateful for.

It was September now. The council vote on the rezoning had gone through as they'd wanted, just over a month ago, and Pixie's home was no longer under threat. There was even better news on that subject, as well.

The car, which Patrick's partially remembered license plate had helped identify as the arsonist's getaway vehicle, had been traced to a part-time employee of Barry Grindlay's through a credit-card receipt pushed under the driver's seat. The man had revealed under police questioning that he'd been paid by Grindlay to set the fire, and the sleazy developer was now awaiting trial.

This should have made Cat happier than it did.

She had finished her eight weeks of practical nursing in the pediatric unit, interleaved with relief shifts at the child-care center. Now she was back to the regular routine of her life. Night shifts at the center several times a week, classes by day, studying when she could fit it in.

She was busy, fell into bed bone-tired every night, but she wasn't happy.

How could she be, when she loved Patrick Callahan, and she'd realized it too late?

Too late? What, was she crazy enough to think now that if she'd accepted his marriage proposal—more like a chess move than a declaration of love—it would actually have led to something? He'd have backed down within days. "Sorry, Cat. You called my bluff. I didn't mean it."

Humiliating.

So at least she had her pride.

And at least she felt confident that she had succeeded in hiding what she felt from those closest to her. This wasn't much cause for self-congratulation, however, as Pixie, Suzanne and Jill were all so deeply caught up in their own concerns. Pixie had Clyde. Suzanne had called recently from New York with the cautious announcement, "I think I've found someone."

"Someone for what?" Cat had asked. She wasn't thinking on her feet these days.

"To marry me, of course," Suzanne had explained impatiently. "To strengthen my claim to raise Alice. Now that Mom has married that awful guy, he's pushing her even harder, and I know he only wants Alice's money. Mom, I'm prepared to give the benefit of the doubt just a little, but not him, only how can I prove that to the judge? But if I'm married…"

"Who is he, Suzanne? Tell me about him."

But Suzanne had refused to give even a single detail. She'd sounded different from usual, too, and Cat was determined to go to New York and see her. Not that this was easy. Her schedule was already packed.

Jill, meanwhile, had left for Montana last week with Sam to organize her divorce. She'd finally gotten time off work, and was determined to be able to give Alan the answer he wanted as soon as possible. Sam had gotten sick when they reached Montana, so her return had been delayed a little.

Alan had dropped in to talk about it with Cat, clearly on edge. "I was the one who insisted she go out there," he said. "This guy in Montana means something to her. That's why she won't give me a straight answer. She says you can't be married to one man and engaged to another at the same time, but that's baloney, isn't it?''

"I—I don't know, Alan. Jill has high standards on issues like that. I thought she barely knew the Montana guy."

"So did I. But believe me, something's going on."

"You're a worry-wart, you know that?" She was beginning to have some sympathy for Alan.

"Yeah." He grinned ruefully. "I know that. But still, I wish she was here. My girls are going wild. They need a woman around."

So Jill and Suzanne were both gone, and Cat spent too much time thinking about a man she couldn't have.

She'd seen him just once since the barbecue at Earl Wainwright's. Pixie had invited him over to English tea, complete with scones and strawberry preserves and whipped cream, cucumber sandwiches and a Viennese chocolate almond torte painstakingly prepared from a recipe in Maida Heatter's *Book of Great Chocolate Desserts*.

The three of them had sat politely sipping and chewing, while Pixie did most of the talking and Patrick and Cat tried not even to look at each other. Let alone touch.

They'd had to talk, though.

He'd asked her about her job and her classes. She'd asked him about his moving plans. He'd sold the luxury apartment without regret, apparently.

"Somehow I just don't want to look at another stainless-steel appliance or granite countertop for a while…"

He was going to rent for a while in New York, he'd said, and next time he bought a place, he wasn't going to get in some expensive designer, he was going to make the decorating decisions himself.

"I like the feel of this place, Pixie," he'd told Cat's cousin. "It's more like my parents' house. It has a warmth to it."

"Wrapped around your little finger and eating out of your hand weren't enough for you, were they, Patrick?" Cat had muttered darkly a minute later, when Pixie was inside preparing another pot of tea. "Now you want her worshipping the ground you walk on, as well."

He had grinned. "Someone should. I was told recently by a woman whose opinion I value that I had a gratuitous streak of kindness in me. Surely that shouldn't go to waste?"

So he'd made her laugh, without her really wanting to. It hurt, and she couldn't think of anything more to say. He hadn't stayed very long after that. Maybe he'd done his duty and had got bored.

That was three weeks ago. He would have moved to New York City by now.

I'll go to New York tomorrow, just for the day, Cat decided. I'll cut classes. I can catch up. I want to see Suzanne.

After all, New York City was a big place. How likely was it that she'd run into Patrick Callahan there? The odds were so small, she had a better chance of winning the lottery.

This fact didn't stop her from looking for him in every crowded New York street. More than once she saw him in a pair of strong shoulders covered by an expensive suit and in the outline of a man's dark head. More than once she heard him in the confident rhythm of male feet on the sidewalk, and in a man's imperious, deep-voiced yell for a taxi outside a gilt and marble lobby.

Her head whipped around, her heart lifted painfully in her chest…and of course it wasn't him. All those foolish times, it was never him.

So she tortured herself by wondering which towering, glass-skinned building held his office, and which riverfront condominium he'd chosen for his rented apartment. She wondered where he shopped and where he ate and if he'd joined a gym and— with a twist in her gut—who he was seeing now. There was bound to be someone.

If Suzanne hadn't been so preoccupied and emotional herself, she'd no doubt have commented on Cat's state. In the end, it was only the two hours Cat and Suzanne spent in the Pediatric Special Care Unit with baby Alice that meant anything and that were able to lift her spirits.

Suzanne held Alice like a mother, her face soft and glowing. She knew every nurse and doctor by name, and every detail of the baby's treatment, routine and progress.

"Alice needs you," Cat told her stepsister.

"You're right. You're the mother she needs."

"I know," Suzanne said, her voice low and intense. "That's why I have to marry Stephen." Two spots of color flooded into her cheeks. "I *have* to!"

Cat envied Suzanne her certainty and understood only too well the intensity of her feelings.

Patrick made a supreme effort to focus on the woman in the room with him, instead of on the woman he couldn't get out of his mind. The one he kept seeing in the streets of the city every time he glimpsed a graceful silhouette and a head of blond hair, every time he heard a golden, full-bodied laugh.

"So," he said, sitting back a little in the swivel chair behind his large desk. "Did you drive up from Philly, Lauren, or get the train?"

He didn't really care about the answer he got.

"I drove," Lauren Van Shuyler answered. She quirked her mouth. "Less time to think."

"*Less* time?"

His attention caught now, Patrick didn't hide his surprise. Lauren was a busy woman. Grooming herself to take over her father's extremely successful home-furnishings empire, she was far more inclined to look at spreadsheets on a lap-top than fashion articles in a women's magazine. As a rule, she'd have seized every precious moment in which to think or work. But she'd changed in some way over the past few months.

Maybe they both had.

A few months ago, Patrick would simply have ignored Lauren's betraying words. He'd have skated smoothly over the slight awkwardness in the atmosphere and proceeded to the business issues she was here to discuss. Now, he decided business could wait.

"Tell me what's eating at you, Lauren," he said, studying her across his desk. "I know your dad's getting worried about you. Now so am I."

He wasn't surprised at what he heard—how she'd found a man she loved and lost him, but couldn't forget the way he'd captured her heart. What he hadn't expected, over the next half hour, was how much he ended up telling Lauren of his own story.

How much he told her about Cat.

And Lauren was a great gal. She really was. He'd had nothing useful to offer on her situation. Even the private detective she'd employed couldn't trace the man she loved, and this suggested to Patrick, in his heart of hearts, that the man himself didn't want to be found. He didn't say so to Lauren that bluntly, but he couldn't think of the right thing to tell her instead.

Despite this failure on his part, however, Lauren had gone on to listen with wide-eyed concern to his own outpouring of the whole truth and almost all of the detail about his relationship with Lady Catrina Willoughby-Brown. Then she had done her best to provide him with some supportive, encouraging advice.

The only problem was, he knew her advice was way off base, and he told her so.

"That's what I tried to do, Lauren," he said. His voice actually cracked as he said it, and he saw her eyes widen in surprise. "That's exactly what I tried to do. All my life that's worked for me. Going after what I want, with no thought in my head at all that I might not get it. Playing to win. Needing to win. Knowing…believing…that I *deserved* to win."

She smiled. "You don't have to tell me. I've seen it, Patrick!"

"And I played it that way this time, too, with Cat. Hell, I blackmailed her and bargained with her and bullied her. Dazzled her, showed off to her, courted her. Only it blew up in my face like a rogue firecracker and that's why I lost her. Pushing like that, playing to win, was wrong. And the only thing that makes sense is to conclude that she was right. We couldn't have made it work. Only it's *killing* me, Lauren. Because I actually, really…'' He hesitated, tried to say "love" out loud, but couldn't. Not to Lauren. He could have said it to Cat, he knew. "…really *want* her now," he said instead, knowing what his heart meant. "It's not about winning any more, not about my stubbornness, or about wanting to prove a point. I don't think it was ever about those things, at the heart of it. And there's nothing I can do about it. She's just not interested.''

"Oh, Patrick," Lauren laughed rather shakily. "How did we each get ourselves into such a mess?"

After this, they went on to talk about the business matters that had brought her here, but she looked thoughtful when she left to go to another meeting, and touched him on the shoulder as he ushered her out the door, instead of firmly shaking his hand as she would normally have done.

"Maybe you and Cinderella aren't done with fairy godmothers, just yet," she said softly.

He didn't ask her what she meant. Her blue eyes were starry with hope, but he was older, more worldly and a lot more cynical than Lauren Van Shuyler. Fairy godmothers, ones that had anything useful to offer, didn't exist.

And he knew when to quit.

The headquarters of the Van Shuyler Corporation took up the top six floors of the corporation's own thirty-story office building in downtown Philadelphia. The rest of the building was rented out by the company to a number of clients, ranging from high-profile legal and accounting firms to management consultancies, a publisher and several retail concerns.

Cat arrived in the lobby of the building ten minutes early for her six-thirty appointment with Lauren Van Shuyler, dressed conservatively, by Pixie's decree, in a knee-length navy skirt and short-sleeved cream knit top. She had no idea what this could be about. She'd received a handwritten note from Lauren herself, on pretty blue stationery, addressed to "Lady Catrina Willoughby-Brown" at Pixie's address.

The contents of the note had been much less formal. "Dear Cat, I'd like to see you about a personal matter. Could you call my secretary to arrange a time to meet with me at my office?"

A slightly cryptic reference to Cinderella, her dress and her fairy godmother completed the short letter and gave Cat an inkling of what this might be about. Did Lauren want Pixie to do some made-to-measure dressmaking for her?

Told about the coming appointment, Pixie had seemed fluttery and a little vague. Really, she hadn't been at all herself over the past few days. There were secretive goings on in her room, and phone calls that weren't explained.

Cat had almost said to her accusingly, "You're not planning to elope with Clyde, are you? Please don't! I'd like to have a wedding in the family to cheer me up. Maybe we all would!"

Because Suzanne had just announced that she'd gotten married in New York last week, with only Rose and Rose's husband Perry as witnesses, and

Jill, who should have been home from Montana by now, flourishing a signed set of divorce papers in her hand, was still conspicuously absent. Alan was threatening to develop an ulcer.

Although she was still a few minutes early when she reached the sleekly groomed offices of the Van Shuyler Corporation, Cat was ushered in to see Lauren straight away. The thirty-year-old business-woman looked different today, dressed for work in an expensive dark red suit with her golden-streaked brown hair folded into a French twist. She came forward to greet Cat, seeming restless. Nervous, even? Cat wondered.

Noting the way Lauren glanced at her watch, Cat apologized. "I'm early, I'm sorry."

"No problem. It gives us more time before—well, it gives us a little time. I—" Again she hesitated, and Cat was astonished. So successful in her professional life, Lauren Van Shuyler didn't seem like a woman who was often struck by such nervousness and uncertainty.

Am I imagining it?

Lauren's next words confirmed Cat's intuition. "Now that you're here, I'm not sure how to do this," she said, opening her hands. "Maybe I should just..."

She didn't finish. Instead, she whirled around and disappeared through a panelled door that led, Cat glimpsed, into the executive bathroom that adjoined this office. She appeared again a moment later holding a dress.

Not just any dress.

It was a wedding dress that was so beautiful Cat gasped when she looked at it. It was made of rich ivory silk embroidered with delicate sprays of flowers in the same pale hue. The bodice was closely fitted, with a ribbing of fine, piped seams. It widened to a shallow, off-the-shoulder neckline and came to a slight point at the waist before dropping into a full skirt, folded into a row of pleats at each side.

There was only one person it could be meant for, one reason for Lauren to be showing it to Cat like this.

"You found him!" she guessed aloud. "Oh, I'm so happy for you, Lauren! You're getting married after all, and you've lost weight over the past few months and you want it altered. Pixie can definitely do it. Patrick may have told you she's a little vague, but when it comes to dressmaking, there's nothing she can't do."

"Cat, Pixie's already altered the dress," Lauren said gently. "It's not for me. It was. It was the dress I planned to wear before I cancelled my wedding four months ago. I haven't found Lock yet—the man who made me realize I couldn't marry Ben—and I'm beginning to accept that I never will find him now. But this dress has happiness written all over it, and it shouldn't go to waste. It's meant for you."

She held it by the embroidered, off-the-shoulder sleeves and pressed it into Cat's arms so that she had no choice but to hold its cool, heavy folds across her body.

"For me?"

"Your cousin Pixie isn't the only one who gets to play fairy godmother around here," Lauren said, just as Patrick walked into the office.

His arrival was punctuated at once by Lauren's assistant, Mary-Jo, closing the door discreetly be-

hind him. He took in the tableau of the two women
and the gorgeous dress with square-jawed, stony-
faced shock.

"What is this?" he growled. "You're getting
married, Lauren?"

But he was quicker to understand than Cat had
been.

"Uh-uh," he went on, after just a second's pause.
"I get it." Now his growl was even deeper, and if
that wasn't anger on his face, then this wasn't a
wedding dress in Cat's arms. "You thought I needed
someone to interfere? I didn't!"

But Lauren held her head high.

"From what you've told me, Patrick," she said,
sounding confident and strong, "And from what I
saw with my own eyes at the Wainwrights' barbecue, the two of you are made and meant for each
other. But I figured neither of you would ever let
the other one railroad you into it, so you needed a
fairy godmother to do it for you. I thought about
kidnapping you both and not letting you go until you
signed the license application forms, but that seemed
a little severe. So then I thought, just the two of you
and a wedding dress together in the same room...."
Tears flooded her blue eyes, suddenly. "Was I
wrong? Surely I wasn't! Don't mess it up. Don't let
the wrong things get in the way. It hurts too much
to be alone when you know in your heart that there's
someone out there for you. I'm sorry, I'm getting—"

She picked up her bag and fled the office, leaving
Cat and Patrick to stare after her for a moment, then
stare at each other in silence.

Cat kept hugging the dress against her breasts and

her waist, as if it offered some kind of protection. Patrick eyed it, his gaze hot and hard. Neither of them moved.

"This wasn't my idea," Cat said.

"I realize that. It wasn't mine, either."

Her heart was beating with slow thuds, her stomach was turning somersaults and she was drinking in the sight of Patrick like a thirst-crazy wanderer in a hot desert. His effect on her was as powerful as it had ever been and her perception was heightened today, seeing him like this without expecting to. She saw that he looked stressed-out beyond his immediate anger. She could swear that he'd lost weight, although there'd never been any spare flesh on that strong frame.

She resisted the need to hit him with a list of questions about his well-being, and managed to say instead, although not as firmly as she wanted to, "There's nothing to keep you here. You can leave. The dress is just a dress. It doesn't compel us to…" She couldn't finish.

Her voice and her body, her breathing and her whole being were radiating everything she felt, revealing it all openly as plain as day. Her jaw had begun to shake and her hands were crushing the silk of the dress like an unwanted sheet of paper.

"It would look fabulous on you," Patrick said, watching her, never taking his eyes from her. "Takes my breath away, actually, thinking about how it would caress your skin and hug you in every place that counts."

"Does it?"

"You know it does. You know it's been that way between us from the beginning."

He stretched forward and touched her face with his fingertips, but she was still too frightened. She ducked the gesture, turning her head away. "Don't, Patrick!" The evasive movement didn't stop her from becoming enveloped in his fresh, masculine scent and feeling his warmth like the pull of a magnet.

"Then your feelings have changed, I guess," he said. There was a scratch in his voice.

"*My* feelings?" she cried out. "You told me I was right before. That you'd only wanted to win. You've moved to New York. It's over. Whatever Lauren thought—"

"Cat, hell, no, it *isn't* over!" he said.

This time, there was nothing tentative about the way he took her in his arms. The dress was crushed between them, a confection of scented silk that rustled against Cat's bare legs and cooled them. They both ignored it.

His mouth claimed hers with hunger and desperation. She was swamped in his familiar onslaught on her senses. His hard warmth, his fresh scent, the slight roughness of his cheek and jaw. The whole world seemed to rock and lose focus. She was light-headed, dizzy, aching, on fire, and had lost all power to take control of this, end it, turn away.

When he dragged himself away from her lips, he laced his fingers behind her head and looked into her eyes, his face blazing with need and certainty.

"It's only over because you told me it was," he said. "That's the *only* reason. You kept telling me, every chance you got, that we were too different, that the worlds we came from were too different. I only ever accepted that because it seemed like you'd never change your opinion. Sure, I handled the whole thing wrong. That stuff about winning. It's a fault, okay? But I realized... I *know*...there's more to what I feel about you, than wanting you as a prize.''

''I—''

He rode over her. ''There's *always* been more, Cat! I just couldn't see it, and neither could you. You, because of the blocks you had, to do with your past.''

''I know,'' she came in. ''I only started to see it on the day of the Wainwrights' barbecue. You told me that stereotyping people because of their situation cuts both ways and you were right. If I'd seen it sooner—''

''No, because *you* were right, also. At first, yes, just like you said, I was only focused on winning. Proving a point. It was about ego and stubbornness and a whole lot of things. I hadn't even realized just how precious the prize actually was. Didn't realize that until I lost it, Cat. Until I made the move to New York and knew that I was never going to see you again. And then it started to hurt so bad that I just hugged it to myself like a kid with a stomach-ache and prayed it would eventually end.''

''Oh, Patrick...''

''Please tell me you can see it now! That you can see what I see about the two of us. I know you do! That you share the same instinct about us, that we're *meant*, we're right and good and strong together. Good for each other. Strong for each other. Tell me that's wrong!''

His voice dropped to a whisper as his mouth came to taste her and tease her and seduce her, confident and gentle at the same time. "Can you tell me that's wrong, Cat?"

"No," she whispered back, closing her eyes and lifting her face to meet his kiss. "No, I can't!"

"I love you. Can't find a way to say it strongly enough. I love you, Cat. Say you love me, too. Say it now, please, if you're ever going to mean it."

"Oh, Patrick, yes. I do. I love you. So much that I didn't dare to let it be real until now."

"It's real, Cat, and this dress is real, and if you'll wear it and marry me in it as soon as we can get it arranged, I'll spend the rest of my life proving to you, in every way I can, just how real it is."

Cat didn't have long to wait. She discovered that there was a lot to be said for winners. They made things happen.

Lauren offered her father's country mansion for the ceremony and reception. Patrick called each guest over the phone and invited them in person. Pixie appointed herself and Suzanne as bridesmaids, and made two beautiful dresses for the occasion in sapphire-blue satin. As Cat had known it would, Lauren's gorgeous silk wedding dress, altered by Pixie, fitted her perfectly. Jill had arrived home from Montana the day before with Sam, and wore a starchy, pasted-on smile all through the ceremony, which Cat planned to challenge her on later.

The Callahans provided a best man—Patrick's brother Tom—and enough other relatives to turn it into a real celebration. Lauren and her father were there, of course, and Pixie's beau, Clyde.

And there in the front row, in the greenery-filled conservatory at Lauren's father's place...were those tears in Councillor Earl P. Wainwright's eyes? In Darlene Wainwright's eyes, too?

"I take full credit for this," Earl claimed extravagantly, once the ceremony was over. "If you hadn't gate-crashed that ball in order to speak to me, Cinderella Willoughby-Callahan-Brown..."

"It can't be a bad omen for married life, can it?" Patrick murmured to Cat late in the evening as they cut the three-tiered cake. "To be watched over by two fairy godmothers and a fairy godfather."

"Not a bad omen at all," she agreed, holding the cake knife as his hand closed warmly over hers.

*　*　*　*　*

*Don't miss the next book
in Lilian Darcy's*
THE CINDERELLA CONSPIRACY
—*SAVING CINDERELLA*
will be out in November 2001.

MAITLAND MATERNITY

You loved
the Maitland
family. Now meet
the long-lost Maitlands...!

In August 2001, Marie Ferrarella introduces
Rafe Maitland, a rugged rancher with a little girl he'd
do anything to keep, including—*gulp!*—get married,
in **THE INHERITANCE**, a specially packaged story!

Look for it near Silhouette and Harlequin's single titles!

**Then meet Rafe's siblings in
Silhouette Romance® in the coming months:**

Myrna Mackenzie continues the story
of the Maitlands with prodigal
daughter Laura Maitland in
September 2001's
A VERY SPECIAL DELIVERY.

October 2001 brings
the conclusion to this
spin-off of the popular
Maitland family series, reuniting
black sheep Luke Maitland with
his family in Stella Bagwell's
THE MISSING MAITLAND.

Available at your favorite retail outlet.

Silhouette®
Where love comes alive™

Visit Silhouette at www.eHarlequin.com   SRMAIT1

Feel like a star with Silhouette.

We will fly you and a guest to New York City for an exciting weekend stay at a glamorous 5-star hotel. Experience a refreshing day at one of New York's trendiest spas and have your photo taken by a professional. Plus, receive $1,000 U.S. spending money!

**Flowers...long walks...dinner for two...
how does Silhouette Books
make romance come alive for you?**

Send us a script, with 500 words or less, along with visuals (only drawings, magazine cutouts or photographs or combination thereof). Show us how Silhouette Makes Your Love Come Alive. Be creative and have fun. No purchase necessary. All entries must be clearly marked with your name, address and telephone number. All entries will become property of Silhouette and are not returnable. **Contest closes September 28, 2001.**

Please send your entry to: **Silhouette Makes You a Star!**

In U.S.A.
P.O. Box 9069
Buffalo, NY, 14269-9069

In Canada
P.O. Box 637
Fort Erie, ON, L2A 5X3

Look for contest details on the next page, by visiting www.eHarlequin.com or request a copy by sending a self-addressed envelope to the applicable address above. Contest open to Canadian and U.S. residents who are 18 or over. Void where prohibited.

Silhouette®
Where love comes alive™

Our lucky winner's photo will appear in a Silhouette ad. Join the fun!

SRMYAS1

HARLEQUIN "SILHOUETTE MAKES YOU A STAR!" CONTEST 1308
OFFICIAL RULES
NO PURCHASE NECESSARY TO ENTER

1. To enter, follow directions published in the offer to which you are responding. Contest begins June 1, 2001, and ends on September 28, 2001. Entries must be postmarked by September 28, 2001, and received by October 5, 2001. Enter by hand-printing (or typing) on an 8 ½" x 11" piece of paper your name, address (including zip code), contest number/name and attaching a script containing 500 words or less, along with drawings, photographs or magazine cutouts, or combinations thereof (i.e., collage) on no larger than 9" x 12" piece of paper, describing how the Silhouette books make romance come alive for you. Mail via first-class mail to: Harlequin "Silhouette Makes You a Star!" Contest 1308, (in the U.S.) P.O. Box 9069, Buffalo, NY 14269-9069, (in Canada) P.O. Box 637, Fort Erie, Ontario, Canada L2A 5X3. Limit one entry per person, household or organization.

2. Contests will be judged by a panel of members of the Harlequin editorial, marketing and public relations staff. Fifty percent of criteria will be judged against script and fifty percent will be judged against drawing, photographs and/or magazine cutouts. Judging criteria will be based on the following:

   - Sincerity—25%
   - Originality and Creativity—50%
   - Emotionally Compelling—25%

   In the event of a tie, duplicate prizes will be awarded. Decisions of the judges are final.

3. All entries become the property of Torstar Corp. and may be used for future promotional purposes. Entries will not be returned. No responsibility is assumed for lost, late, illegible, incomplete, inaccurate, nondelivered or misdirected mail.

4. Contest open only to residents of the U.S. (except Puerto Rico) and Canada who are 18 years of age or older, and is void wherever prohibited by law; all applicable laws and regulations apply. Any litigation within the Province of Quebec respecting the conduct or organization of a publicity contest may be submitted to the Régie des alcools, des courses et des jeux for a ruling. Any litigation respecting the awarding of a prize may be submitted to the Régie des alcools, des courses et des jeux only for the purpose of helping the parties reach a settlement. Employees and immediate family members of Torstar Corp. and D. L. Blair, Inc., their affiliates, subsidiaries and all other agencies, entities and persons connected with the use, marketing or conduct of this contest are not eligible to enter. Taxes on prizes are the sole responsibility of the winner. Acceptance of any prize offered constitutes permission to use winner's name, photograph or other likeness for the purposes of advertising, trade and promotion on behalf of Torstar Corp., its affiliates and subsidiaries without further compensation to the winner, unless prohibited by law.

5. Winner will be determined no later than November 30, 2001, and will be notified by mail. Winner will be required to sign and return an Affidavit of Eligibility/Release of Liability/Publicity Release form within 15 days after winner notification. Noncompliance within that time period may result in disqualification and an alternative winner may be selected. All travelers must execute a Release of Liability prior to ticketing and must possess required travel documents (e.g., passport, photo ID) where applicable. Trip must be booked by December 31, 2001, and completed within one year of notification. No substitution of prize permitted by winner. Torstar Corp. and D. L. Blair, Inc., their parents, affiliates and subsidiaries are not responsible for errors in printing of contest, entries and/or game pieces. In the event of printing or other errors that may result in unintended prize values or duplication of prizes, all affected game pieces or entries shall be null and void. **Purchase or acceptance of a product offer does not improve your chances of winning.**

6. Prizes: (1) Grand Prize—A 2-night/3-day trip for two (2) to New York City, including round-trip coach air transportation nearest winner's home and hotel accommodations (double occupancy) at The Plaza Hotel, a glamorous afternoon makeover at a trendy New York spa, $1,000 in U.S. spending money and an opportunity to have a professional photo taken and appear in a Silhouette advertisement (approximate retail value: $7,000). (10) Ten Runner-Up Prizes of gift packages (retail value $50 ea.). Prizes consist of only those items listed as part of the prize. Limit one prize per person. Prize is valued in U.S. currency.

7. For the name of the winner (available after December 31, 2001) send a self-addressed, stamped envelope to: Harlequin "Silhouette Makes You a Star!" Contest 1197 Winners, P.O. Box 4200 Blair, NE 68009-4200 or you may access the www.eHarlequin.com Web site through February 28, 2002.

Contest sponsored by Torstar Corp., P.O Box 9042, Buffalo, NY 14269-9042.

SILHOUETTE *Romance*

COMING NEXT MONTH

#1546 THE MISSING MAITLAND—Stella Bagwell
Maitland Maternity: The Prodigal Children
A mysterious man rescued TV reporter Blossom Woodward—and then kidnapped her! Blossom's nose for news knew there was more to Larkin the handyman than what he claimed…was he the missing Maitland they'd been searching for? Only *close* questioning could uncover the truth…!

#1547 WHEN THE LIGHTS WENT OUT…—Judy Christenberry
Having the Boss's Baby
Scared of small spaces, Sharon Davies turned to a stranger when she was stranded in an elevator, and got to know him *intimately*. Months later, she nearly fainted when she met her boss's biggest client. How could she tell Jack their time in the dark had created a little bundle of joy?

#1548 WORKING OVERTIME—Raye Morgan
Temporarily sharing a house with a woman and her toddlers awoke painful memories in Michael Greco, and sharing an office created more tension! The brooding tycoon tried to avoid Chareen Wolf and her sons, but eluding the boys was one thing—resisting their alluring mother was more difficult….

#1549 A GIRL, A GUY AND A LULLABY—Debrah Morris
A friend was all aspiring singer Ryanne Rieger was looking for when she returned to her hometown broke, disillusioned and pregnant. She found one in rancher Tom Hunnicutt. But Tom wouldn't be content with *just* friends—and could Ryanne ever let herself give more…?

#1550 TEN WAYS TO WIN HER MAN—Beverly Bird
Sparks flew the moment Danielle Harrington and Maxwell Padgett met. Strong willed and used to getting her own way, Danielle tried everything she could to make successful and sophisticated Max fall for her, except the one thing guaranteed to win his heart: being herself!

#1551 BORN TO BE A DAD—Martha Shields
Good Samaritan Rick McNeal became a temporary dad because of an accident. When Kate Burnett and little Joey needed a home, the lonely widower opened his door—but would he ever open his heart?

RSCNM0901